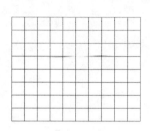

The Pornographer's Poem

American Whiskey Bar

Kingsway

Hard Core Logo

Company Town

8

MICHAEL ✕ TURNER

10

DOUBLEDAY CANADA

Doubleday Canada and colophon are registered trademarks.

Library and Archives of Canada Cataloguing in Publication has been applied for.

ISBN: 978-0-385-66593-3

This book is a work of fiction. Names, characters, places and incidents are products of the author's imagination or are used fictitiously. Any resemblance to actual events or locales or persons, living or dead, is entirely coincidental.

The author wishes to thank the Canada Council for the Arts for their economic support during the writing of this book.

Printed and bound in the USA

Published in Canada by Doubleday Canada,
a division of Random House of Canada Limited

Visit Random House of Canada Limited's website: www.randomhouse.ca

10 9 8 7 6 5 4 3 2 1

For Judy

The young lordling once went out walking full of thought and came to a well. He looked into it and in the mirror-clear water saw his donkey's form.

"The Donkey," *Grimm's Fairy Tales*

It is related that a pair of tricksters once saw a simpleton leading a donkey by its halter along a deserted road. "I will steal that beast," said one of them to his companion, "and make an ass of its master."

"The Donkey," *The Arabian Nights:*
Tales from a Thousand and One Nights

8

×

10

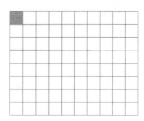

By the time he was sixteen his thighs had become so developed from speed skating his father had to make his trousers for him. These were the days when trousers were pants, made of denim or twill. Fashionable pants fit tight at the waist and loose below the knee, where they flared like muskets, swallowing the clogs that were also in fashion.

The pants were called bell-bottoms, and they were made by the newer companies, the most popular brand having an explosion on the right back pocket. Older companies remained competitive, but they serviced the uniforms of bikers and greaseballs—those who preferred their legs straight, their pants jeans.

With money saved from his paper route, he purchased a denim pair, asking that they be let out here, he pointed, and here, too, Dad.

His father bundled up the denims and left for work.

That evening, while preparing supper, something caught his eye. His first thought was to collapse, curl up in a ball, like he did as a kid when his father came at him.

He turned to find his father hovering in the hallway. His father had been doing that a lot lately—hovering—and it was beginning to get on his nerves.

[8×10]

Hey, Dad.

His father stepped forward, unfurled the denims.

He did his best to look thankful. His father had taken material from the bottom of the legs and reapplied it to the tops, thus defeating the purpose of bell-bottoms.

The next time he bought bell-bottoms he took them apart himself. Using newspaper, he made a pattern, then added the inches needed.

Again he showed his father, and again his father left for work. Only this time, instead of alterations, his father returned with a modified version of the template: stovepipes, not bell-bottoms.

As before, he did his best to look thankful.

He knew his father was frustrated, so he asked if he could help. Together they would make his pants.

His father nodded.

By day's end, both men were satisfied. The only things missing were the pockets.

His father picked up some scraps and began cutting.

Let's just use the store-boughts, Dad.

His father eyed the store-boughts, the one with the explosion.

I mean, why waste the material?

Why waste the scraps? his father shot back, grabbing the pockets and pinning them to the seat of his pants.

A few months later his father made a new pair, recycling the pockets from the last ones, now faded. The reproach was not lost on him.

That summer he gave up speed skating. By winter his legs had returned to normal. Bell-bottoms by then were passé.

His father continued to make his trousers. Not denims but wool dress pants, the kind he wore to work, like everybody else.

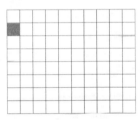

She hated the city. Hated everything about it. The people, the buildings. *Everything.*

It had been ages since she spoke to someone. That kid with the dog, its head the size of a boulder.

Spare some change, ma'am?

Fuck off.

She would have slapped him if not for that dog.

She spent her days at the kitchen table, a co-operative building just east of the downtown core. She drank tea, read the paper, wrote poems in the margins. Children ran past, screaming, grabbing what they could off the counter. Not even hers! No idea whose.

(Hers had grown. But they were not hers either. Not really. Not *legally*. Plucked from her breast the day they were born.)

She pined for the north. The mountains, the forests, the slow, winding rivers. And the old plank store, where everything hung from the ceiling. Point and they would take it down for you, wrap it up nice in brown paper.

She bought her mother's housecoat there. White flannel, with red and yellow roses. Her best day ever was walking home with that bundle under her arm, the snow in the mountains, the afternoon sun igniting its peaks.

Pink tits, she wrote. And the sky behind it/ a light blue shirt.

It was marriage that brought her here, a marriage that lasted just long enough to disqualify annulment. Nine months is too many, said one expert. Think of the child, said another.

She shut her eyes, let her pen drop.

And the sky behind it/ a faded denim shirt.

It had been wartime. The northern landscape was changing. Forests were being razed, fences unspooled, roads imposed. Even the newspaper looked different: the type was larger, and every day more pictures than words. She noticed these things. Then the soldiers.

They started showing up at dances. Always a big commotion, people rushing to the windows, the bus that brought them as clean and shiny as they were.

She did not care for them at first. (Nobody cared for the

soldiers, least of all the men.) But one stood out, and he pursued her, convinced her she was different.

(That appealed to her—being *different*. All her life she had been told she was beautiful. But *how* beautiful? And to *whom*?)

He was by far the most handsome man she had ever seen. And it startled her, her feelings for him. So she left the dance hall early, walking home with the woman who sold pie.

For the next six days he was all she could think about. The width of his shoulders, his long, wavy hair. When she saw him again, he offered her his arm. Without thinking, she took it.

He was a good dancer. Graceful as a river/ solid as the oaks that lined its shore. After their second dance he asked if she would join him outside for some air.

Until then she had only kissed two boys. The first a stiff peck, more innocent than clumsy, a cousin. A year later, the cousin's friend, someone she met on a hike. The pack out of sight, he lunged at her, his tongue splashing in her mouth like an eel. Unbearable.

But the soldier's kiss, his was like the ocean fish swim in—rolling, flowing, abundant. She could feel herself sinking, taking on water. She reached for his shoulders, pulling him towards her, her feet off the ground, dangling.

The last time they met he was waiting for her behind the hall. They had decided to skip the dance and walk to the river, together.

She had been rehearsing the moment for weeks. Everything—every move, every breath—had been imagined.

He would tell her he loved her, and that he wanted to be with her, forever. She would take the pendant from her neck, the one her mother gave her, and drop it over her shoulder. Then, taking his hand in hers, place it on her breast. He would kiss her first, before squeezing.

Which he did.

[8×10] How she ended up over that rock is a mystery, a consequence, she later wrote, of a poor imagination. Not a bad feeling, but not a comforting one either. For it is the sequence that baffles. His lips where his hand had been, his hand in new places. Then hers detaching, turning animal. How he took it, wrestled it, pressed himself against it.

She opened her eyes, squeezing.

A flashlight to someone who had only known matches.

But there was no penetration.

When he came, the volume was so great she thought for sure she was pregnant.

But how? There was no/ penetration.

The next day he shipped out.

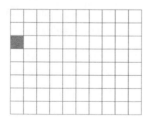

She was astonished to learn of her son's test score. Does this mean he should be enrolled in a special school?

The principal smiled. We are prepared for such contingencies. As we speak, a tutor is being arranged.

She asked a second time, to make sure she had heard right.

He assured her. One hundred and fifty-one. Genius.

She was full of questions, but he was already on his feet, ushering her out the door, past the secretaries, down the locker-lined halls, congratulating her on her son's genius, telling her again and again what an honour it was to have a kid like him in their midst, and that he would be in touch, thank you for coming, goodbye.

Back at his office, the principal buzzed the secretary in charge of petty cash. No sooner had she closed the door behind her than he asked for sixty dollars. She returned with the cash, along with a form. He signed the form and handed it back to her. Along with the cash.

She was confused.

Sit down, he said. I have a proposition for you.

She was new to the country, having arrived with her husband six months earlier. Back home she was a speech pathologist, and he a doctor. But because their adoptive country did not recognize their educations, they took what they could get. She found something right away—school secretary—while he held out, eventually surrendering to split-shift dishwasher.

Now, for the first time since emigrating, one of them was being offered something substantial.

The principal asked if she would be interested in tutoring a gifted student two days a week. She would be paid thirty dollars an hour; at the end of the month, there would be an assessment.

Without thinking she accepted. The extra money would go a long way.

One more thing, the principal added. We'll just keep this between ourselves, for now. He leaned forward and whispered, I don't want the other girls thinking you're above them.

[8×10]

The thought had not occurred to her, but now that he mentioned it . . .

Where do you come from? asked the boy.

Same place as you, said the tutor.

We all come from the same place, said the boy.

The tutor hesitated. Where did you learn to talk like that?

The boy shrugged.

A month later, the tutor met with the principal and the boy's mother. The tutor's presentation was long and elliptical, much of it lost on the mother, whose facial expressions ran the gamut from appreciation to fear. As to why the boy's class-work was average, the tutor said her pupil was operating at a higher level, and that the classroom was too slow. She finished with a cardboard model made up of seven triangles, based on the boy's thought patterns, his way with words.

There was a pause at the end. All eyes were on the boy's mother.

So what you're saying is, my son's a poet?

Not a poet—a jack of all trades! declared the principal.

Not a jack of all trades, said the tutor carefully, but a poet first. A metaphysician.

The mother brightened. We've always wanted our son to be a doctor.

Meta, said the principal, means everything.

Meta, said the tutor, from the Greek, meaning with, after. Denoting a change of—

Do you think he's ready for university math? asked the principal.

The tutor frowned. I would not encourage him in that direction.

Why? asked the mother.

The boy is strong, mathematics will soften him. His gift is poetry.

The principal appeared concerned. Can't he be both—a poet *and* a mathematician?

Of course, said the tutor, but a poet first.

In his heart, said the mother, smiling.

Yes, said the tutor, in his heart.

At the principal's recommendation, the boy would now receive daily tutorials. In addition, he would give a recitation of his poems at the winter assembly. (Also on the bill, a tap-dancing juggler and a girl who could bounce two basketballs at once.) The boy's mother was delighted. The tutor said nothing.

The following day, while sifting through her folder . . .

What are you looking for? asked the boy.

Nothing, replied the tutor.

Nothing as in zero?

Nothing as in this stupid recitation. I think it's belittling. Performing on stage with clowns.

The boy frowned. I wish I could bounce two basketballs at once.

Any monkey could do that, said the tutor.

Then I want to be a monkey! said the boy.

She found what she was looking for: an envelope from the school's testing agency. She had sent them a letter, and now, two weeks later, their reply.

[8×10] The boy leaned towards her. I said, I. Want. To. Be. A. Monkey.

Her suspicions were confirmed. There seems to have been a mistake, she told the boy. You scored 115, not 151.

The boy shrugged. Anything over eighty is an A.

A for average, said the tutor.

M for monkey, said the boy. Oo-oo-oo!

She smiled. She liked the boy. He made her laugh. We'll just keep this between ourselves for now.

For now! said the boy, leaping from his chair like a monkey.

The extra money had improved her situation. Her husband no longer had to work nights, and she could send something to her mother. Losing the income would mean her husband would return to nights, and her mother, who could finally afford to send letters, would lose face with the postmaster.

A couple of days later, when the principal was at lunch, she snuck into his office and peeked at the test scores. She was astonished to learn that the mistake lay not with the testing agency but with the principal.

It had been her experience that conceited men did not like having their mistakes pointed out to them. Pointing out the principal's mistake would probably cost her her job—and then where would she be? On the other hand, she could give her student the best education possible, and none would be the wiser. The boy had potential. If he was not a genius, at least he was different.

She would wait the weekend.

With his nights free, her husband had time to study for the exam that would allow him to practise medicine in their new country. Not only that, he had taken an interest in cooking, preparing the lunches they took with them on their walks. A favourite walk was to a park at the opposite end of town, a marshy corner where they kicked off their shoes and ate.

She had just unfurled their blanket when, out of the corner of her eye, she noticed a couple stepping from behind a large bush. It looked like the principal and his wife. But as the couple moved closer, it became apparent that it was not his wife but her pupil's mother.

Thinking quickly, she told her husband she had dropped her comb, and to wait while she doubled back to find it. Once the couple passed, she returned, holding up the comb. Although not out of breath, her heart was racing.

It was the beginning of the school week, and still she had not made up her mind. Seeing the principal with the boy's mother only complicated things. As she made her way up the school steps she realized that her best course of action was to take no action at all. It's just a job, she kept reminding herself. Show up, do the work, go home.

No sooner had she opened the office door than she noticed two uniformed policemen standing at her desk. One tall, one not so tall. Behind them, the principal. And behind him, the other secretaries.

There she is, said the principal, that's her.

The taller cop stepped forward, unhooked his handcuffs and began reading her her rights. On her desk, arranged in a grid, the petty-cash forms, some of which had zeroes added. The charge was theft.

She felt nauseous; one of her knees buckled. There's been a mistake, she pleaded, I didn't steal anything, I've never stolen anything in my life!

Suddenly a calm came over her. She looked the principal in the eye and said, I can't believe you'd do this. What have you got against me?

The principal turned to her co-workers. She could not hear him, but she could read his lips: See what I told you? Next thing you know she'll accuse me of adultery.

The secretaries nodded. Then, as if a whistle had blown, they returned to their desks, in silence.

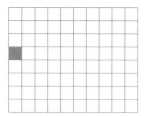

It was taking forever. In and out of the bathroom, reinserting his catheter. His mood was not helping.

No big deal, he kept saying. I don't care if they come.

But he cared. And she knew it. And he knew that she knew it.

She was on her knees, picking at his laces. He had insisted on tying them himself, and now she had to use a pin.

Means more to you than it does to me, he continued. I'd be just as happy if they cancelled.

She got to her feet. No you wouldn't.

Yes I would! he bucked.

The phone rang. She left to answer it.

Above his headboard, a rectangular window. If he were standing he would have a view of seven tree-lined ridges winding their way down to a silver strip of water. But from where he was sitting, all he got was the weather: a flat grey monochrome.

Inspired, he took the pen and pad from his night table and began to sketch the ridges from memory. He was doing well until his eyes started to hurt. Not the sketching but the thinking behind it.

When she returned she got him to his feet, his chicken legs shaking. Here, she said, placing his hands on the bedpost. When the wheelchair touched the back of his legs, he sat.

Like a trained animal, he thought.

On her knees again, lifting one foot onto the footrest, then the other.

Don't know why they're doing this now. Could've used it forty years ago, when I was insecure, he said with a laugh.

She was staring at him.

What?

You're drooling. I'm gonna have to change your shirt.

He wiped his chin against his shoulder.

She opened the closet door. That was the reporter calling. She said she's running late. Asked if noon's okay.

Noon! Day's half-done by noon!

He liked the shirt she picked out. Big collar, puffy sleeves. He had seven more just like it. He reminded her of that, but she knew.

She started from the bottom, one over-starched button-hole to the next. He enjoyed her hands in his lap like that. Felt good having more than a catheter down there. Next time his shirts went out, he would ask for more starch.

She was two buttons from the top when he realized how much his neck had shrunk.

Take it back, he said, it's too big.

I would, she began, but your tailor died five years ago.

He knew that too. Forty years with the same guy, then all of a sudden . . .

She opened his tie drawer. Red or yellow?

I'm no coward, he muttered.

Pardon me?

Red, he said.

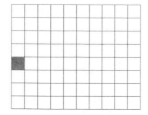

She could count on one hand the number of times she saw her father growing up. Her sixth birthday, and the dog her mother refused to let in the house; her first year at high school, suspended for stealing a muffin; graduation, and the picture she carries of the two of them standing stiffly by his car.

She had been thinking about him a lot lately. Where he was, what he was up to. And in doing so it occurred to her that, although he never gave her anything (at least nothing she could hold in her hand), he always left something behind. Like the replacement present, after her mother said no to that dog.

If ever you find yourself in a situation where it's you or them, hold your hand like this. And he demonstrated, holding his hand flat, like a ping-pong paddle.

She did the same, as did the other kids sitting cross-legged around him.

Now, with all your might, hit him—here! He grabbed her hand and held it to his windpipe. Somebody screamed, and her mother, who had just stepped outside with her birthday cake, told him to get the hell out—now!

Only when she did something wrong did his name come up. And even then it was never spoken. If you don't smarten up, young lady, you know what I'll do, don't you? I'll send you to live with you-know-who!

Not that she believed her. She did not believe anything her mother had to say. All she believed in was getting through life with as little hassle as possible.

Which is why she lied about the muffin.

She knew her father was behind on his child-support payments, and calling it a whim would only make matters worse. So when he asked her why she took it she shrugged and told him, I was hungry. Unfazed, he turned to her mother. Can I have my daughter for the day? To which her mother replied, Don't stop there—you can have her for good!

[8×10]

Next thing she knew the two of them were in a cab, her father telling the driver to drop them at a thrift shop just east of the downtown core. He wanted to teach his daughter a lesson.

The thrift shop belonged to a charity. Inside were three middle-aged ladies in smocks and gold bracelets, one of them bossing a handicapped man.

She had never been to a thrift shop before. Nor could she understand why anyone would wear something that belonged to a dead person.

But her father was not interested in clothes.

Clothes up front, he said, speeding down the aisle, books in the back.

The bookshelf was four rows high and five feet wide. Above it a cardboard sign: ALL BOOKS A QUARTER.

He got on his haunches and pulled out a hardback. He began to flip through it when something caught his eye.

Jackpot!

She leaned in: a drawing of a car part.

He looked at her. Doesn't look like much, does it?

She shook her head.

Nice drawing though, huh?

She shrugged.

It's a starter motor. He shut the book, turned it over. In excellent condition.

Their visit to the bookshelf lasted less than a minute. Two volumes on mechanical engineering, three children's pop-ups and a novel whose back flap featured a white-haired woman in cat's-eye glasses. Grand total: buck fifty. While paying he asked her to go outside and hail a cab. She was surprised how much fun that was. [17]

Their next stop was an apartment above a butcher shop. An older woman answered. It was well past noon, but she was still in her housecoat.

The woman lit up when she saw them, announcing her father's name like he had just won a prize. Then, turning to his daughter, she asked, What's it like having a man like this for a dad? Isn't he marvellous!

She felt there was an answer—a funny one—but all she could come up with was a shrug.

The woman's apartment was filled with books—books against the walls, on tables, the floor. The only place without books was the window overlooking the street. If only to remind myself where books come from, said the woman as she opened a tin of cookies.

She sat at the window, pretending to read a book on horses while her father and the woman chatted. Although she had problems following their conversation, the details told her more about her father than anything her mother had said. Not that they talked about themselves, or each other for that matter.

From what she could gather, her father travelled a lot. When he was younger he used to jump trains, but nowadays he spent most of his time in a car, selling industrial equipment, sometimes staying on to show people how to use it. He had just returned from a town where a friend was working, someone the woman knew well. He told three little stories about this man, and after each the woman shouted the man's name like she had her father's earlier. The girl was not sure why, but it made her jealous.

She shut her eyes. The image that came to her was of her father and the woman driving down a country road. It was winter, late morning, the sun low on the horizon. The car was filled with cigarette smoke. A thermos of coffee between them.

To strangers they might seem like mother and son. But if they looked closer, they would see that the woman was not much older. Neither old enough to be his mother nor young enough to be his girlfriend. But friends all the same. Close ones.

He finished with a joke, and the woman laughed so hard her housecoat fell open. She was shocked to see how young and fresh her breast looked—as young and as fresh as her own. It was then that her father picked up his books and placed them on end. As if on cue, the woman donned her glasses and assumed a frown.

If her father was fast, the woman was faster. The books barely touched her hands as she checked their date of publication, condition, things her father would explain in the cab, fifty dollars richer.

When he was not talking about books he would scribble on the back of an envelope the names and addresses of dealers, who they were, what days they reserved for buying. As they pulled up to her house he reminded her that if she was ever stuck for money she would do well to visit thrift shops, and not steal muffins from school. She nodded, gave him a peck on the cheek, then ran from the car in tears, the list on the dash where she left it.

By the time she was sixteen she could not go an hour without using. If asked to partake in something longer, she would refuse. She had no choice.

A week before graduation she asked the valedictorian the length of his speech. When told he was still working on it, she promised him oral sex if he could keep it short. From what she gathered, the principal's address and the conferring of diplomas never took more than thirty minutes. So forty minutes max. That she could do.

But something happened—a last-minute guest. A famous actor married to someone's sister. The principal asked if he might say a few words, and the guy gassed on for an hour. Not that she lasted that long, slipping out halfway, headed for the bush where she stashed her rig.

As she was crossing the parking lot, who should she see but her father, chatting with one of the chauffeurs.

Hey, there's my baby now! he said, stepping towards her. But the look on her face slowed him. Are you okay?

She told him she had her period.

Oh, well, this shouldn't take long. He went to his car and retrieved his camera, asking if the chauffeur minded.

You're cold, he said after the first flash.

I'm losing blood, she lied.

He took off his jacket, hanging it over her shoulders like a stole. Better?

Yes, she said, but not before noticing the scars on his arms.

[8×10] The camera snapped a second time. But this was not the photo he sent her mother, the one the girl took with her when she left.

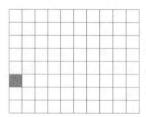

Before she made beer rep, she worked in pop. Her job was to find out where the kids went, then show up with surveys and promo. First to finish won the cooler, the next three received T-shirts, the rest got to keep their pens.

It was easy at first. The beaches were teeming, one of the hottest summers on record. Back up the van and the kids would come running.

The problem was the survey. The company was only interested in teenagers, and you had to be at least thirteen to fill one out. No survey, no promo.

This angered the younger kids, and some of them got surly. Usually the teenagers would shoo them away, but one of these kids threw a rock at her, chipping her tooth. After that, the lifeguards told her to keep it in the parking lot, where the real consumers were, in cars.

Then the weather changed, and the kids went back to school. Her first impulse was to set up outside the record stores. Which she did, until the cops demanded a permit. She tried the community centres. Same thing. Fortunately she had befriended some of the younger kids and, being younger, they knew everything anyway. Ice rinks after school, bush parties at night.

She learned a lot from these experiences, and they served her well when she went for beer rep.

Her trapline consisted of the waterfront bars. The company cautioned her, urging her to team up with someone on the west side first, someone with more experience (for less pay, of course). But she said no, she liked the challenge. Plus she wanted the big bucks.

So off she went, in the truck she bought with her pop money, to the toughest bars in town.

Her first stop was a windowless concrete box wedged between a gas station and an auto wrecker. Above the door shone a blue and red OPEN sign. Inside, three men dressed in coveralls sat slumped against the bar. Behind the bar, in a black leather vest, the bartender. She introduced herself, and he ignored her.

She tried again.

This time the bartender looked her in the eye. You're no beer rep, he said—you're not even old enough to be here! C'mon, let's see some ID.

She reached for her wallet, then hesitated. If I'm not old enough to be here, then you're not a biker. Because if you were a biker, you'd be out on your hog right now, not working some shit-ass job like this, huh?

The men at the bar took notice.

Shit-ass job! said the bartender, stepping out from behind the bar. Shit-ass job!

[8×10] She held her ground. Guess my age and I'll give you ten cases of whatever you want, gratis.

Ooooooo, gratis, said a voice from the bar. Isn't that foreign for fuck my ass?

Laughter.

Not for nothing it isn't, she shot back.

Oooooooo . . .

Watch her, said another voice. She's good.

The bartender looked her up and down, paying special attention to her neck and hands.

The look of experience, she told the men at the bar. Someone who knows how to tell time.

I'm warning you guys, said the second voice.

The bartender held up his hands: two Vs for victory. Twenty-two! he roared. She's twenty-two or it's fake ID.

At first the company was concerned. She was giving away too much premium beer, especially to bars whose stock-in-trade was draft. But after a month the orders started rolling in.

Marketing, of course, took notice. Premium sales contradicted the demographic trend: years of union bustings had caused wages on the eastside to decline, and overall sales were down. When the senior westside rep was promoted, he offered her his old job. But she declined, saying she was happy where she was. She did ask for a raise though, and he gave it to her.

The story gets told like this:

Chick walks into a bar, says she's a beer rep. The bartender says, Forget it, let's see some ID. She lips him off, then says, I'll promo you ten cases of whatever you want if you can guess my age. Bartender looks her over, looks at her neck, looks at her hands, then says, You're twenty-two. The look on her face! She makes a phone call and thirty minutes later—ten cases of import! Everyone gets a round, gratis. Funniest thing I've ever seen. I mean, the look on this chick's face!

Here is another version:

Not long after I became CEO we hired a young woman two years out of high school as beer rep. Until then, her only experience had been soda pop demos. Our plan was to pair her with someone experienced, then, if she worked out, let her loose on her own. But she wanted to dive in, so we gave her the toughest bars in town.

After six months she increased premium sales by twenty-five percent—this despite a slumping economy. Her method was simple: she would ask bartenders to guess her age, and if they guessed correctly, she would promo them ten cases of import. If they didn't, well, it never came to that, because everyone's a winner with this kid. Some guessed nineteen, others twenty, twenty-one, twenty-two . . .

Great gales of laughter, followed by a steady stream of applause.

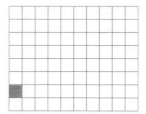

[8×10] The story of how her life was saved and how it differed from those in the crowd. For she was neither poor nor disenfranchised. Nor had she been abused.

It was the day of her promotion. She was driving home, in the middle of the bridge, when suddenly, out of the corner of her eye, a woman swings one leg over the guardrail, then the other, and jumps. All in one quick, deliberate motion.

She could not believe it. Something she ate—food poisoning—or a hallucination. No one else could believe it either, they kept on driving.

But it was real, she decided, so she pulled over and called the police. The dispatcher told her to exit the bridge and that an officer would be by to take her statement. Which he did, though not before giving her a ticket, for stopping.

Every day for a week she called the police station, and every day they told her no, they had not found a body, eventually telling her to stop calling.

It got to where she could no longer concentrate. Her colleagues complained, her clients grew frustrated, even her boss expressed misgivings. Maybe you're not ready, he said.

Then she had a dream.

The dream begins the day of her promotion. She is

hovering above her cubicle, watching her co-workers as they stop by to congratulate her. Although happy on the outside, she feels uneasy, as if something were alive at the pit of her stomach. Something angry.

She follows herself to the elevator, to her car, then the middle of the bridge, where, as if a cloud had just passed, she finds herself staring back at where she last looked down. Swinging one leg over the guardrail, then the other, she jumps.

Lights swirl, the cold air nips at her face. She fights to keep her head up. When she hits the water, it is stomach-first, and she explodes in five directions. Out of which comes a new self, a lighter, more vaporous self. Like the self that followed her to the bridge. In a language she has never heard before, she is told to wake up, and what to do upon waking.

It is 3:17 a.m. A choir is singing. Which is odd, she thinks, because her alarm is set on newstalk. Rising from bed, she goes to the closet, not knowing what she is looking for until she finds it. The scrapbook she made with her mother.

She turns the glue-heavy pages, eventually stopping on a drawing of a man in white robes and beard. Above him, a thought bubble. I HAVE NOT SENT HIM INTO THIS WORLD TO BE ITS JUDGE, BUT ITS SAVIOUR. This, too, is strange, because the handwriting belongs neither to her nor her mother.

An hour later she calls in sick. The following day, the same. Then the day after that. And the day after that. Until the seventh day, when she quits altogether.

Upon telling her story, someone would invariably ask: What did you do before you were saved? And because she tells the truth, she tells them advertising.

Then the hands go up. Kids are fascinated by advertising. They know it is manipulative, but because they are manipulative too, they want to know how it works.

So she tells them.

[8×10] One of the first rules of advertising, she begins, is to create a need. You have to convince people they need something in order for them to buy it. And the best way to do that is to give it away. You've heard the expression, The first one's free?

Laughter.

Next thing you do is come up with a snappy name, something memorable, a word or a phrase you can repeat without feeling embarrassed. Like a car named after a horse, or a weapon. Something masculine. Attach to that a sexy image, and voila, there you have it!

Before I was saved, all I cared about was money, making as much of it as possible. In my first year I doubled the company's accounts; in my second year, I tripled them. It got to the point where I could sell piss to the breweries. But it's meaningless unless you believe in something higher. Drugs can get you there, but only for a moment. He can last all night.

He.

He was her product. He, or him, depending on the construction. Always uncapitalized, unless at the beginning of a sentence.

Get it? she would say after writing his name on the blackboard, and they would nod, mouth it to themselves. He.

The secret of her success, she believed, was confession, her belief that honesty negates the means. It's not as simple as apples versus oranges, she would say. Nor is it sweet versus savoury. It's a big step, the biggest you'll take. But the rewards are huge, like long underwear on the coldest day of the year, or a glass of water on the hottest. You have no idea how good it feels. All you have to do is open yourself up—believe—and he will fill you, completely.

But no matter how much he filled her, she never got over what happened on the bridge that day—and the dream that followed. Wasn't he supposed to take care of that? Wasn't he supposed to take that hole away?

One morning, after a particularly fitful sleep, she got up early and walked to the bridge. The sun was an hour from rising. Cars whizzed past, and it had begun to pour.

At the spot where the woman jumped, she closed her eyes and recalled her shape: slender, average height, drab clothes. She never saw her face, only a quarter profile. Her hair was dark, her lips full and parted.

One leg over the guardrail, then the other, gone. All in one quick, deliberate motion. Is that how it's done? No hesitation, no last look? Had she tried it before? And if so, how many times until she got it right?

What was going through her head?

She put her hands on the guardrail, leaned over the water, and spat—a small white dot spiralling into the black pit below.

Useless, she said to herself, letting go with another drop of spit.

Useless.

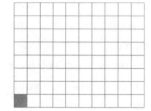

[8×10]

What kept her eyes open was not the muscles in her head but an interest in everything about her. Every day something new, or something she knew from the day before. Stare at it long enough and her hand would move; only when touched would it come into focus. If it was not accompanied by volume, she would touch it again. Touching something twice plus volume was to know what it meant to ignore it, and never again would she touch it.

There were times of darkness and two times of light. Sometimes inside there was no light, except the light from the outside, which she preferred. It made her happy, sleepy, though not enough to stop her.

Outside light was sometimes shade, yet she knew it connected to the warmth she preferred. Not what went whoosh when the house turned on but touch from the ball in the sky.

Softly it came, in patterns, making everything more than it was without. When it was not shade, outside light had a different skin, and sometimes it was too much. She would move, always to where it was not. Given less room meant she was bathed in the light inside, where she slept.

Places were not on or off, nor were there two kinds of off. There was movement from behind the outsides, like the house turning on, and the night coloured thing with bells that stopped when it touched a head. The box with the world inside and boxes that called without pictures. And the room where the tweet lived, until one day it lay still, after which it was taken down and disappeared, with nothing to hang in its place.

Sometimes form would fall, and the place it made from breaking went from things she could see through, though sometimes made from dirt. Like the bowls she saw in the room that buzzed, bowls from which others filled their mouths.

And her own place, the place that came to her as if pressed against, busy with stuff going in her. She could barely breathe, which made the volume of her body go. Only then did it feel better, or the way she felt before.

The place she reached for was water, not the tap but the rooftop when the light went shade, the tapping falling water makes. Her arms would rise and she would think of the pipes outside, the water dropping down them like the waters inside her.

The taste of what went in, neither hot nor cold but the same as her. The taste made it better, and for that reason she never stopped. She kept on not stopping until she could not breathe. The place her throat made, and what came out, which was how she knew she had had it.

Once, after the waters fed, and the rooftop raised her, she discovered a tall dirt bowl stuck with outsides. She touched it, and had no thoughts. Yet the next time she touched it what should come at her but places—a dot the colour of an outside, getting bigger, then falling, the way waters do on outsides when not on the roof. There was movement, more than usual, and a place that made more waters. Her hand was taken from her, and the volume that resulted was more than pain itself.

Mouths in her face, round places filling the bowls inside her. Some more powerful than others, as if the holes above her mouth saw too. She was removed, held against. Indoor light and more round places. Only one mouth now and a tweet wasting the same thing over and over, above her head, like the boxes that called without pictures.

It was not like her, not like the other tweet, because this tweet was too shiny and had no waters. She did not have to touch it to know that, she just did.

Darkness. Not from disinterest, but the weight of the bowls inside her, pulling her down, tucking her into spaces she never knew. What stood out, what she had to touch twice, and what was touched twice. She arranged these things inside her, but was not happy with the arrangement.

So she returned to what she knew, making her insides rooms. Beside the window, a tall dirt bowl with outsides. The light she chose was not yet shade, nor the light which made her move from. There was movement, some soft round places and the room that buzzed warmth in the holes. The tweet, before it lay still, and what it did with its arms, the way everyone moved just like it. Their unround places, similar to the first tweet. Then new places, like the places she made when her waters ran.

She was alone, allowed to touch whatever she looked at. It went on this way until she was moved to the room where the waters lived, the great big bowl and the waters that brought volume to her eyes every time she opened them. She wanted the tweet, the first tweet. She made places in her mouth until she was brought the new one, the one that hovered above her.

More places now, in new ways, using parts she had not known. They took her to a room where the first tweet lived and sat her on the floor, mouths open. She looked about her. Nothing she had not touched before. Her arms hanging there, dead beside her.

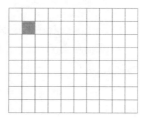

For the past ten years he received in the mail a calendar from the company he spent over half his life working for. The calendars had notes attached, holiday greetings from the gals in the office. How's the handicap?! How's that backhand coming along?! Friendly stuff, but inaccurate: he hated golf, and he gave up tennis after the war.

The calendars were landscapes, and went right into the bin. But the notes had a way of sticking around, popping up on cupboards, the refrigerator—he even found one under his slipper. He had no idea how much he would miss their insincerity, until they stopped coming.

As it happened, the company had merged with a competitor. There were layoffs, including the gals in the office. Not that anyone had told him—he only found out during one of his daughter's occupations: the invasion of his kitchen in the name of brunch.

It was a ritual he endured, one he fell into after his wife died: his son-in-law hiding behind the newspaper, his daughter at the stove, scrambling eggs, while his grandsons surfed the linoleum.

His son-in-law looked up from his paper. According to this article, your company's problems began over twenty years ago.

Even his grandsons could do the math on that one.

Any idea how it might affect your pension? the son-in-law added.

His daughter tossed some tomato slices into the frying pan. Dad doesn't need his pension, do ya, Dad?

He had invested wisely.

Dad?

I'm ten cents away from having spent your inheritance.

She giggled.

His son-in-law turned the page.

It made him nauseous to eat with his grandsons. Anyone's grandsons, for that matter. He recalled how proud he was when, after years of segregation, his father invited him to sit at the big table. You have excellent table manners, his father told him. Good boy.

He was eight at the time, two years younger than his daughter's eldest, a feather-headed rock star who cut his meat with a spoon.

His daughter glanced at his plate. Not hungry, Dad?

You need to eat, keep your strength up, chomped the son-in-law, his mouth a yellow hole.

Dad! cried the youngest, exposing his own hole. Grandad says don't talk with your mouth open.

Good boy.

After brunch, they moved to the living room. From his chair he could see his grandsons in the backyard: the youngest picking petals off a cosmos, the rock star tossing handfuls of gravel at the neighbour's dog.

His daughter refilled his teacup. How's your health, Dad?

Neck surgery, he joked, had given him a new leash on life.

But it was his memory he was worried about. There had been incidents. Not that he let on.

Because we were wondering, added the son-in-law, looking around the room, maybe this is getting a bit . . . I don't know . . . a bit *big* for you?

What do you mean you don't know? he thought to himself. Of course you know! He took a sip. Why, am I shrinking?

His son-in-law was never right, nor would he allow it. But sometimes he was close, and this was one of those times.

Since his wife's death he lived almost exclusively on the main floor. He could not remember the last time he visited the basement, nor pulled a weed from the garden she so carefully maintained. Watching it grow over had become a source of shame.

I've been thinking of moving, yes.

Good news! clapped his daughter.

Any idea where? asked the son-in-law, barely able to contain himself.

I've had my eye on a complex.

She looked concerned. Not far, I hope.

I know the developer, he said he'd give me a deal.

They listened.

The move was relatively painless. After deciding what he needed—his desk, his chair, some books and photos—he gave what remained to his daughter. What she did not want she sold to an agent. What the agent did not want was left to the son-in-law to dispose of.

He settled in easily. The residents were professionals mostly, all of them retired. Doctors, engineers, a couple of professors. There was the odd goofball, but they were benign, more amusement than nuisance.

He spent his mornings walking around the marsh; in the afternoons he napped. Twice a week he played billiards in the common room, a former farmhouse on which the complex was themed. When not reading, he watched television, though not as much as the others, the blue glow a ubiquitous sight when returning from billiards.

It was during billiards that he heard a familiar voice. But

before he could turn around, How's that backhand coming along? One of the gals from the office. She was moving towards him, in full bloom. Remember me, or have you gone ga-ga too?

Without missing a beat—and for reasons unknown to him—he replied, It's true, I have gone ga-ga. But I'm still breathing, and if you come a little closer, you'll know how hard.

The room collapsed in laughter.

Fanning her face, she responded, Why yes, and quite quickly at that!

More laughter, but from the men only.

Not since the war had he felt so invigorated. The next thing he knew they were strolling towards the marsh. Conversation had slowed; there were breaks. He felt nervous, like a kid on a first date.

Up ahead was a huge round rock. He imagined her lifting her skirt, bending over it.

She nudged him, Know what I mean?

He did not—he was lost again—but said yes anyway.

Pardon me? she asked.

Nothing, he said. Carry on.

She had bought into one of the newer subdivisions. A smaller unit, she said apologetically, as if twelve hundred square feet were the wrong side of the tracks.

It bothered him that she alluded to their material differences. Never once did he think of her as one of "his" secretaries, former or otherwise. Especially now. But her confidence returned once the topic shifted. She had neck problems, too, but was getting results with acupuncture.

Her townhouse was at the other end of the marsh, a mile from the common room. They arrived at her gate in no time.

He opened it.

She invited him in for tea.

Her unit was sparsely furnished, without the oppressive knick-knackery that dominated many of the suites he had visited. She favoured landscape photos over paintings, chairs over loveseats, rugs over carpets. The walls were grey. Her tea set simple yet elegant.

He took a sip, returning the cup to its saucer.

I heard your wife passed. She touched his hand. I'm sorry.

He reached for a biscuit. She went fast. No pain. He took a bite.

I've always liked you, you know. You always treated me nice. She gave his hand a squeeze.

He smiled. Then suddenly he had no idea where he was. I feel the same, he said.

As if a fish had jumped. Suddenly her hand was on his knee. Then let's do something about it!

He felt a stir. Fear, pleasure? He was not sure.

Can you still get an erection? Because if you can't, I have pills.

Things were moving too quickly. He reached for his cup, more to steady himself than to sip from.

Her hand was on the move again. And just so you don't get the wrong idea, I'm not in it for the money, you know; I have investments.

Good god, he thought, would this woman just shut up!
She smiled. So what's it gonna be?

He bit into his biscuit, chewed a little. Tell me about
these pills.

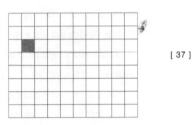

His boss was incredulous. Pills! he kept saying. Pills!

He looked at his feet.

I give you a jimmy—I teach you how to jimmy—and you
come back with . . . pills?

There wasn't any jewellery, so I thought—

You thought! Under his breath, so his protégé could hear
him, Stupid fuckin' monkey.

The wind had died down and the air in the shack was
still. Here, he said reaching into his pillowcase and pulling
out a vial. The suffix tipped me off.

The suffix! His boss grabbed the vial.

The suffix, things that end in ene mean—

I know what ene means, his boss said, tossing the
vial aside. He took a cigarette from his shirt pocket.
A train sounded. He lit up, exhaled, then sat down on the
corner of a large wooden crate. I want you to do something for me.

Sure, anything!

I want you to take some of these pills.

Where?

No, I want you take them—as in swallow them. And after you've swallowed them I want you to write down what they do to you.

He nodded eagerly.

[8×10] That way we'll know what we're dealing with, how much to charge, et cetera.

So we can sell them, he told his boss.

Right, so we can sell them, make some fuckin' money. He pushed off the crate, sweeping aside the blanket where once there was a door.

It had stopped raining. The sun was out and the trees were steaming. Who knows, said his boss, stepping onto the plank walkway, we might be onto something.

He followed, careful not to step in the muck. Yeah, I was hoping—

You know much about drugs? he interrupted.

No, not really.

Ever take them?

During the war we took speed. But other than that—

Any speed in your pillowcase?

I don't know. But if I had to guess, I'd say it's mostly downers.

He stopped. What's the suffix for downers?

Pardon me?

Well, if ene means uppers, how do we know when something's a downer?

Uh . . .

He slapped him on the back. Just monkeying with ya!

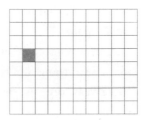

She was depressed. She tried to hide it but he knew her too well. Pretty soon he was all over her.

What the hell's the matter with you? Why are you being such a jerk?

I don't know, just tired I guess.

They were in the kitchen, sitting at opposite ends of their new antique table, a thermos of tea between them. She was doing her best, but he kept at it.

That reporter's been phoning again. I thought you were going to take care of it.

She got up, started walking. No idea where, just walking.

Look at you—you're walking in circles!

She went into the bedroom and flopped onto the bed. If she were standing she would have a view of seven tree-lined ridges winding their way down to a silver strip of water. But lying there, all she got was a light blue monochrome.

He stopped in the doorway. You haven't been the same since the robbery.

She said nothing.

A month earlier, while at the hospital, a kid broke into their basement and ran through the house. Total unprofessional, the cop said. A roll of pennies, a letter opener, medicine. Probably trying to impress his friends, was the cop's opinion.

But it was not the theft that bothered her, it was the intrusion. Everything he touched she wanted thrown out. Underwear, dresses, one of which was torn, as if he had tried it on.

Transvestite kid, the cop said.

What if the thief was a girl? she asked.

The cop scoffed.

She offered her dress size, thinking it might help, but the cop put his pad away, said they would catch him eventually.

She looked up.

He was beside her, staring.

What?

Cherry or lemon?

Cherry or lemon what?

In his hands, a white bakery box. He opened the lid, and on the other side, a drawing of her holding a battle-axe. Cherry or lemon danish, he said, smiling.

What makes you think those colours mean those flavours?

Fine, he said, tossing the box aside, be like that.

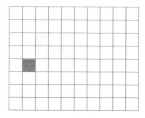

Sir?

He had forgotten where he was.

She cocked an eyebrow, clicked her tongs. Your order?

A bakery. He was in a bakery. Right, he began, three of the cherry and three of the lemon.

Bag or box?

Box, he said, taking an envelope from his pocket and jotting down the make, model and colour of the car across the street.

Nice day, huh?

Still jotting. Sorry?

The weather, said the girl.

He looked outside. It was raining. Oh, you're being sarcastic!

Duh.

Ah, you're doing it again! Very funny. Or should I say, funnier? He put the pen back on the counter and returned the envelope to his pocket. Quickly, what's your favourite sex position?

Ew, gross! said the girl, but still smiling.

No, it's a joke. Say anything.

She looked him in the eye, her hands on automatic as she tied the box shut.

He noticed the scars on her arms.

Seriously, I have a daughter your age. We kid like this all the time.

The box secured, she wrote the price on top. Okay, she said sheepishly, from behind.

Pick you up at eight!

Ewwwwwww!

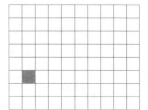

[8×10]

He stopped what he was doing. Whaddaya mean, Ewwwwwww? That's not what you say when somebody takes off their shirt, Ew.

Yeah, but not everyone has a scar like that.

He looked at his chest.

High-side yer bike or somethin'? Sure doesn't look like an operation.

With his finger he traced the cord of flesh from sternum to abdomen, around his hip to his buttocks, stopping where he would need a mirror to see the rest (up his back, an inch from his spine).

Fine if you don't want to talk about it, she said, unhooking her bra. No skin off my ass.

Nice.

She lifted her breasts, the nipples staring back at her. Yeah, she said smiling, I like my tits. So do the punters. I reckon I've sold more—

No, no, no. Not like that. Not like *babies*—here. He stepped towards her, gesturing. Let 'em go.

She did.

Yeah, like that. Just hangin' there. Yeah. He took them in his hands and felt their weight. The untanned parts, the contrast. Like night and day, he said. He brushed the nipples with his thumbs, and they stiffened.

She reached for his belt buckle. Whatcha got on tap, barkeep?

And the colour, he said. What colour would you call that, your nipples?

[43]

She laughed, took a step backwards, her smile perfect but for a chipped front tooth.

Yeah, like that.

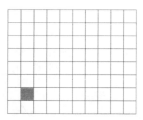

She could hear him in the kitchen, coughing, the tinkling of his belt. Would he say goodbye? He did not seem the type.

He was not coming back.

From her pillow she could see his bike, yellow under the bug light. Appropriate, she thought. He calls it a hog, but to her it looks more like an insect, a wasp. A few hours earlier, outside the bar, she watched him mount it, his leg swinging over its thorax, how good it looked.

Would he start it, or would he roll it to the end of the block? That would be the considerate thing. The cowardly thing.

He was supposed to be different! But what does that mean—*different*? Different from what? Everyone was different these days.

On the nightstand was a box of matches. She took one, rolled it between her fingertips, then held the explosive end under her nose. She liked the smell. Different from lighters.

With her thumbnail she struck it. She imagined the shadow behind her blooming. Not from her head but what it looked like on the inside. Her thoughts. Ghosts.

The flame was halfway down when she remembered her cigarette. She lit it, took a drag, then dropped the match down a pop can. Tsss.

Just as well, she thought. He wasn't that good. Yes, he had potential, she would give him that. Or maybe it was the other way around: potential was his to give. Maybe that was it. Maybe that was the difference.

People kept telling her how similar they were. The first time she saw him she was startled. Not by his looks, but how well these people knew her.

She liked the way he moved. He could have been a dancer. Maybe he was and was keeping it to himself. Maybe in another life, like her.

Her friends waved him over. It took a while before she could look at him, really look at him. Slender, average height. His hair was dark, his lips full. Like hers.

They spoke of their childhoods, what they had in common—growing up in a family business, how difficult it was to find time alone. When the band kicked in, they left.

The pipes shuddered. He was at the sink, the echo of a plastic cup bouncing off the tiles.

He would need her help. The door was broken, and she had been using an ice pick. Would he call for her, or would he figure it out on his own? Depends on how patient he is. A frightened man might go crazy once he realized the windows were barred.

She braced for his entrance. Nothing. Another cigarette. Still nothing. She put on her T-shirt and was about to call out when something told her no, not yet. He was not ready. He would need more time.

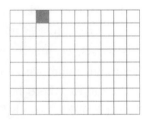

While walking home from school it occurred to him that the day his body stopped growing was the day he would begin to die. He announced this at the dinner table, the way children do at a certain age, once they realize their proclamations get more attention than their questions.

His father motioned for the hot sauce; his mother passed it to him.

You'd better have another one soon, the boy added. I'm not gonna be around forever you know.

His mother glanced at him. Don't say "you know" at the end of your sentences.

He looked at his father.

His father looked up. What?

You know what I'm talking about, said the boy.

He was an only child. There was another but she died at birth. Something to do with his parents' blood, the way it mixed. That was what they told him. Not his parents but his teacher. An only child herself.

His father never cried over his sister's death. If he did, he kept it hidden. But his mother, she cried for days. Judging from their arguments, it seemed to be her fault. Nothing was ever his fault. At least not from what he gathered.

His mother worked nights. As soon as she left, his father was up from his sewing machine, muttering, scratching at his wrists, eventually bursting into the boy's room and beating his bum with a hairbrush.

It got to where he could not sleep until he had his beating. Which is why he acted out. Nothing hurt more than being beaten for no reason—except lying there waiting for it to happen.

He would cry. Not the pain so much as the look on his father's face, like a mask, like he was not even there. He would shut his eyes and pretend to be elsewhere; running through brambles, canoeing down rapids, re-entering the Earth's atmosphere at a thousand miles per hour.

Sometimes he could not help it. Sometimes he caught a

glimpse of his father's face, and it burned. Only later, after it evaporated, could he reach inside himself and turn off the tap, poke at his buttocks, check to see if the skin was still taut, if it stung. If it was—if it did—he knew that that would evaporate too.

On the inside of his closet hung a mirror. When they moved in his mother tried to pry it loose, move it to her room. But the clips were old, and she feared it would break. Instead, she told him she would visit when she needed it.

Which she did, every night, putting on her makeup, swatting at her hair. Or sometimes in the mornings, waiting for the tub to fill. But over time the visits decreased. He assumed she was bathing in the afternoons. It had been ages since he had seen her naked.

When she first started using the mirror he was full of questions. What are you looking for? What are you looking at? Rarely did she answer. If she did, she was impatient, or absent altogether. Only later did he realize that whatever his mother was doing was between her and her body; it had nothing to do with him. So maybe it was he who was absent. Maybe it was a dream. He was never sure.

After his beating, he would wait for his father to start snoring before sliding out of his pyjamas. Once naked, he would light a candle he kept in his closet, then stand before the mirror and touch himself, the way his mother did, looking over his shoulder at the redness of his backside, how similar it looked to the stuff she put on her cheeks, how his body resembled hers.

His mother's body was small and compact, his father's long and thin. Because of his gender, he assumed he would grow up to look like his father. But lately he was not so sure. His face was getting broader, and his feet had grown pudgy like his mom's.

The last time he saw his father naked, he noticed how much fuller his penis was in proportion to his body than his father's was to his. Which seemed odd, because the first thing he noticed about his mother was that she did not have one.

It frightened him that he would have his mother's penis.

Then he remembered something he had heard in science class: how baldness is linked to the mother's father. Therefore it made sense that he would have his mother's father's penis. Not that he had seen it. The only flesh he had seen of his grandfather, besides his face, were his hands, which, now that he thought about it, looked more like his mother's sister's than his mother's. Confusing.

He was glad to have something in common with his grandfather, and nothing with his father. He liked his grandfather more than anyone. And now they shared a secret.

His grandfather visited on weekends. If his legs were hurting, he would spend the night. One day he came home from school to find his grandfather sitting at the kitchen table, staring out the window.

Grandfather!

Although excited to see him, excitement on this day was mixed with dread. Something bad had happened. Or was about to. He could tell.

Where're my parents? he asked.

His grandfather smiled. They have some business to attend to.

When will they be back?

I don't know, he said. But what I do know is there is some ice cream in the refrigerator, and we should eat it.

Weird, he thought. Ice cream was for special occasions, and although his grandfather's visits were always special, he would never mistake them for special occasions. Something was up. His grandfather opened the carton, and he could feel the cold air rush across the room and slap him in the face, bringing tears to his eyes.

It was his grandfather who taught him how to reach inside himself and turn off the tap. But this was different. This time it would take both their hands.

He ate quickly, hoping the ice cream would give him a headache, distract him. He was halfway through his bowl when he put down his spoon, went to his room and sat on his bed. A few minutes later his grandfather joined him, telling him stories of the towns he had visited and the people he met there. Like the cook who sang for a whale, and the parrot who recited recipes. But he had heard these stories before, and his mind began to wander.

Bath time! he announced suddenly, leaping up from his bed.

Don't you have your bath before you go to sleep? asked his grandfather.

No, said the boy, pulling off his T-shirt, I'm usually too tired. I have my bath in the afternoon, like my mom.

Well, said his grandfather, getting to his feet, you're a big boy now.

He kicked off his trousers and went to the mirror. I've grown a lot, haven't I, Grandad?

You certainly have, said the man, making his way to the door.

The boy pushed down his underpants and closed his eyes. Grandad, I need to ask you something.

After your bath, he said over his shoulder.

I need to ask you something now. He opened his eyes. It's important.

His grandfather stopped, scratched at something above his left eye. Can't it wait?

He sensed his grandfather's discomfort. He had seen it in others, the way feelings get trapped under the skin and make you itch. His father did something similar when his mother asked him not to touch her, or follow her to work—things he did not have words for—just before she smacked him.

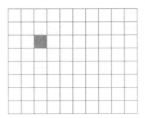

It was a long voyage, a week longer than advertised. A rough one, too. Many died, one of them an hour into the journey.

They tried to keep the body cold by pressing it against the ship's walls. But by the third day it reeked so bad she could stand it no longer. A deal was struck between her husband and a crew member—they would be relocated, in exchange for services rendered.

As they neared port, she asked her husband where he went at night. Wait until we've landed, he said. Then I will tell you.

[51]

She wanted to insist, be the kind of wife who demanded—and got—answers. Like her mother, who only had to look at her father—or any man for that matter—the baker, the postman, soldiers—and they would submit. But something about his tone, the construction of his response. She decided to respect his wishes.

They had been ashore six months, and still the topic had not been broached. Then one day, while sitting down to a picnic lunch, she asked him, and he had no idea what she was talking about.

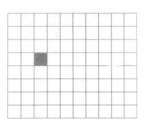

It was decided, even before he knew what a decision was, that when he grew up he would become a doctor, a specialist. And that is what happened. But like many specialists, he had other talents. In this case, an ability to render, quite accurately, whatever was put before him.

When he was eleven he drew a picture of a beggar who lived in a box at the end of his street. One of his teachers thought so highly of the drawing that he entered it into a competition. During the adjudication one of the judges, a local official, recognized the beggar's nose as the nose of a war criminal, a man responsible for the deaths of hundreds of people. So accurate was the rendition.

[8×10]

Police were dispatched. They kicked down the boy's door and demanded that he take them to the beggar. When the boy asked why, one of the policemen grabbed him by the neck and shook him so hard he wet himself. The boy asked if he could change his pants first—and for this he was punched in the face. No more pussyfooting around! said the cop.

After his nose had stopped bleeding, the boy took the police to the end of the street. But when they got there, no beggar. No box either. Enraged, the cop who had grabbed him earlier pushed him against the wall and accused him of criminal interference. When the boy asked what criminal interference was, the cop began strangling him, and his co-workers had to pull the man off. An argument ensued, with one group insisting that the boy be charged with conspiracy, while the other, noticing that their shift was up, wanted to break for dinner.

The argument spilled onto the road, with the policemen eventually disappearing into the crowd. But the boy did not wait to see this—he was already on his way to the opposite end of the street, where the beggar was sitting in his box, fixing the brakes of his wheelchair.

The police are looking for you, said the boy.

No big deal, said the beggar. I don't care if they come.

The boy was incredulous. Aren't you scared?

The beggar wiped his brow. Whatever I've done is a matter of opinion, nothing more.

Years later, while his country was being ravaged, the boy, now a respected urologist, had a chance to move his family to a place where war was unlikely. But it would not be easy. [53] Because of his political connections, he and his family had become the opposite of anonymous. Someone would recognize them. And if they were caught, they would be killed.

A deal was proposed. In exchange for descending the testicle of a plastic surgeon's son, the urologist and his family would be given new faces. But they would need papers too, so the plastic surgeon sweetened the deal: kill her husband and dispose of the body, and the surgeon, who was also a talented forger, would supply them with passports and visas.

This was the deal they shook on, and how they left the country.

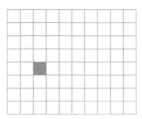

It never occurred to her that her parents came from somewhere. Only when assigned their histories did she give it much thought. Yet the more she thought about it, the more she realized it was not something they wanted to talk about. Even without asking, she knew.

She was an only child. There was another but he died at birth. Something to do with her parents' blood, the way it mixed. Or so she was told. Not by her parents but by someone at work. A customer. An only child himself.

[8×10]

Maybe that's why they split up, because of your brother.

He was an older man, though she never thought of him that way. To her, he was in-between. Not her father, but not a schoolboy either. Someone special. Someone she visited with every time he walked through her door.

Even at her busiest, she always made time for him. If not in words, then in noticing things. A new coat, the colour of his scarf. One time he wore sandals and she could not keep her eyes off the length of his toes. A haircut was a special occasion.

And he noticed her too. One afternoon, while reaching into the display case, she caught him looking at her bum. It took everything she had to straighten herself. Words lie, but the eyes—never.

It was an odd feeling, one she could not shake. It sat behind her on the bus ride home and watched from the television as she fed her cat. It even followed her to the bathroom, where she exchanged her uniform for the T-shirt she slept in, its neck stretched wide from tossing and turning. This feeling of something coming.

While crashing around her room one night, she noticed herself in the closet mirror. What he might have seen earlier:

a girl bent over, reaching for something. She shut her eyes but it was too late—she could resist no further. Gravity tugging at her, angry with her, done with her for good.

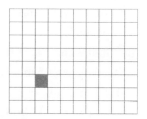

As soon as he left she noticed his satchel. She was about to chase after him but curiosity got the better of her.

From her window she watched him get into his car, pulling out once the traffic eased.

Inside the satchel she found a toothbrush, a bunch of pens and a notebook filled with writing.

The next thing she knew she was reading.

He had been looking for someone. An ex-girlfriend he dealt drugs with at the bar. She was behind on her payments, and if she carried on the way she was headed, she would be killed.

So he put the word out. Not that he was looking for her, but that he was using again. The next morning he got a call. Come on over, she said, we'll get you fixed up.

The fence around her property was a palisade, an inch under code. To get inside you had to go around back. At knee-height, a hole with a wire sticking out. Pull the wire, push the board.

Once inside you had ten seconds to get to the basement door. After that, the dogs were on you.

Inside the door was a workshop. Beyond that, another room, in the middle of which sat an old man behind a desk. An order would come in, and he would make up a package. The package, like the order, was relayed through the house by dumbwaiter.

[8×10] To the right of the workshop was a flight of stairs.

He found her in the kitchen, huddled in the nook. She was wearing a housecoat decorated with red and yellow roses. Her hair looked like a cross between fibreglass and cotton candy. She was staring out the window, smoking.

She turned to him. Wanna see how we get the dogs in?

He shrugged. Somewhere along the way she had lost her front teeth.

Coffee?

Sure.

A boy of about sixteen, wearing only a T-shirt and bracelets, jingled past.

Milk and sugar? she asked.

Black, he told the boy.

The view outside was of seven ridges. Three had been logged, the rest covered in half-built mansions.

The grinder startled him. He turned around. The boy had one hand on the grinder, the other on his ass, scratching.

She nudged him. Sick, huh?

Pardon?

She pointed out the window. Used to be forest down there, now it's castles.

He nodded.

Down by the water, that's where they cook this shit up. Them and their lawyers.

Things change, he said.

She looked at him sharply. Things and people. She dropped her cigarette into a pop can, gave it a shake and returned to the window. You've aged, she said.

He shrugged. What can you do?

About what? she asked the window.

He thought for a second. About what they're doing down there, the developers, he replied.

She smiled. I've been putting some thought into it, and you know what I've come up with?

No.

See that face up there?

He nodded. About a mile away, eight hundred feet of sheer granite.

Couple sticks of dynamite—boom!—it all comes tumbling down. And then her laugh.

The kid was at the table, holding out a plate of cookies. She took one.

How long had it been? he wondered. And this kid, was he her lover, her son?

She bit the cookie in half. Do you like boys? she asked him matter-of-factly.

He lit a cigarette. I'm not here for boys.

She returned to the window.

After coffee they fixed. A few long words and he found himself in the dining room. His clothes were off and he was lying by the window.

Outside was a magnolia. The wind had picked up, and on the wall behind him, a complicated dance of shadow and light.

The shadows conjured something. A building inspector torn apart by dogs, a rockslide stopping just short of a mansion.

He was drifting off when suddenly he felt nauseous. He went looking for a bathroom. The one on the main floor was plugged, so he went upstairs.

Through a half-open door he could see her, reflected in a mirror. She was naked, leaning over a chair, the kid crouched behind her like a dog. There was a groaning sound, but it was coming from the walls, not them.

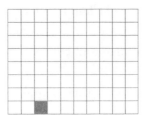

Doctors told her recovery takes time, prepare for the worst.

Her physiotherapist said recovery is not a return to something but a becoming of something else.

A nurse who had worked in palliative care advised her to give up who she thought she was and get acquainted with her new self: a cross between the person she wanted to be and the person she would most likely become.

Easier said than done.

She had no idea what had happened to her. Nobody was talking either. When you're ready, they kept telling her. When you're ready, we'll tell you.

When you're ready, when you're ready.

Some things she did know. Like the seriousness of her situation. How she was rushed to hospital, how her surgeon kept quitting on her—the last one stepping from the table and announcing that he had done everything humanly possible, that the rest was up to her.

They were amazed she survived the night.

Once stabilized, her needs were minimal. But she had them. Administrators too—they needed her bed. A social worker was assigned. He studied her file and eventually located her daughter, who took her home.

She is not sure the exact moment she regained consciousness. There is an official time, but it can't be right, she kept thinking, because she remembers things from the day before. Whether these were things told to her, or dreams, she is unsure. All she knows is that it took a while to convince herself that heaven is not her daughter's sewing room, and that nowhere in death does it say you will not want a cigarette.

Consciousness is not black and white, she once read, and there are no exact moments. But she thinks she might have dreamt that too. Nothing is for certain, they kept telling her; and this, she decided, is how people articulate hope:

because we are imperfect the news is never as bad as it seems.

But it was not just herself she was worried about, it was her daughter too. A month after moving in she discovered her daughter had a drug problem, and that she was selling her body to pay for it.

Her daughter's life had changed, and it continued to change at a rate greater than her own. So she left. There was no other way. If she stayed, she would not improve. And she had to. Because who would look after her daughter?

[8×10]

There was insurance, a portion of it going to a small apartment just west of the downtown core. Her daughter, convinced her mother would never regain consciousness, sold her possessions, so of course she needed new ones. A bed, a dresser, a table and chairs. She even bought a car, although she was miles from driving it.

Some of the money she would give to her daughter, to be disbursed at intervals, some of it went to clothes. But nothing fancy. Practical stuff. Shoes, coats, underwear, a pair of jeans she could garden in.

She loved jeans. Always had. As a child her mother forbade her from wearing them, but eventually gave in. She remembers the first time she tried a pair on, the way they fought back. But more than that, how her ass felt. Secure, protected. Dresses left her exposed, vulnerable. She had been raped while wearing one. But this was years ago, a time she chose to forget.

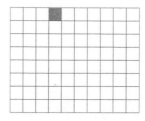

The moment he was born he knew his son would never cut cloth. When they held him up, the first thing he noticed, besides his sex, was his hands. And because they were his hands, he knew his son would suffer.

He would never cut cloth. Nor would he measure, sew or point to a crotch and ask, Which side? He would distinguish himself in other ways. Someone who signed his name for a living, someone important, not some poor arthritic tailor.

When his son was eight they gave him a test. A week later the principal phoned.

His wife answered.

Can we meet?

Everything changed after that. Appointments with tutors, experts—all of it falling on her because she worked nights and he was too shy. It got to the point where they only saw each other at supper.

Not that she complained. At least not often. But when she did, he was there for her, telling her it will be worth it, our son will go to college, be a success—a scientist, a poet, whatever. And she would smile, collapse against him, sometimes touch his arm.

Every week he put money aside.

Someone important
with people under him
a boss

was his mantra.

[8×10] But as the years passed, so did his son's potential. School bored him. Eventually he lost interest, and his tutor was reassigned. Most of his time was spent at the rink.

He wanted to be a speed skater. But instead he became more like her: obsessed with his body, how it looked, its surface. A matter of time before he runs off too, he thought.

Which he did. After graduation. Gone. No idea where. The whole summer—not even a phone call.

When he returned, he was flush. Money for the first time in his life. He did not know how much until he peeked in his closet: under the carpet, beneath the floorboards, an envelope stuffed with fifties.

Where did you go?

I got a job.

Where?

In government.

Where in government?

Can't say. All I can tell you is my work is sensitive.

The father believed him. Until he found the fifties.

The next morning he got on his bicycle and followed his son to work—a warehouse east of the downtown core. An hour later his son emerged, dressed in coveralls; him and two others. They climbed into a truck and headed west down an alley. He gave chase until he lost them on a hill.

It was midnight when his son returned. He was waiting for him in the kitchen, the newspaper open, the radio blaring. A bank manager had been shot in the face, while a teller was in hospital, fighting for her life.

Terrible, his son said, brushing past.

He got to his feet. What do you know about it?

Grabbing a pear from the counter, I was driving by when they caught him.

What do you mean *him*? There were three of them. And they're still at large!

Biting into his pear, You calling me a liar?

Don't talk with your mouth full!

Answer the question.

How dare you talk to me like that—I'm your father.

He watched as his son sauntered down the hall. When he got to his door, he pointed to a spot just below the knob. I put a hair there, now it's gone.

All night long he tossed and turned. Twice he thought he heard him, but it was mice. When he was certain, he went to the window—and there was his son, racing across the yard.

His movements were odd. Someone taught him to run like that. Someone had trained him.

The father secured the house, bolting the doors and windows. Then, reaching under the sink, he removed a box reserved for rags. On the bottom, next to a pistol, lay her diary, right where she had left it.

He sat at the table and turned the pages, reading not what was written but the shapes the words made. What was recorded quickly, in darkness, what was laboured over, and why.

When he could read no longer he went to his son's closet and pulled up the rug. A shoebox this time, filled with fine white powder. He knew what it was, just as he knew the consequences of having it. He considered flushing it down the toilet, and would have had his son not returned.

Dad, let me in! he yelled, pounding on the screen door.

What do you want?

I forgot something. He reached for the handle and waited for his father to undo the hook.

Incredible, he thought, not only does he look like her but they have the same way of reaching for things.

C'mon, Dad, open the door. He gave the screen a shake.

Deceitful too. Then, angrily, You don't work for the government, you're a criminal, a crook!

Aw c'mon, Dad, not now.

Don't Dad me, you're not my son!

Okay, you're not my father either. Fuck you!

Like a punch in the gut. Everything slowed after that, everything except his hands . . .

C'mon, Dad, I was only kidding.

. . . hanging there.

He pointed at his son's ring. You know, the day will come when that won't come off.

A siren.

It was her father's ring, and when the light was right, it shone like nothing else.

He took a step back, raised his foot and . . .

Like a star, bursting.

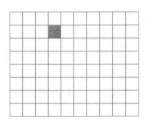

Basic training was not what he expected. Rumours of sadistic drill sergeants and young hearts exploding over obstacle courses were just that.

He did not sleep the night before. All he could think about was stepping off the bus and getting frogmarched to the barber, a three-second haircut and a uniform thrown at his chest.

As it turned out, the opposite was true. The crowd greeting them looked more like camp counsellors than drill sergeants. None had crewcuts. One had hair to her ass.

They were their hosts, as they preferred to be called, and after organizing them into teams, they were led to barracks and assigned beds. Not the rickety bunks from movies, but doubles covered in cloud-like duvets. At the foot of each, a hamper, compliments of the company that had the most to lose if the war they were waging went south.

After dumping their gear they were encouraged to look around, get to know each other. At one of the buffet tables he asked a host when they might be getting their uniforms. The host laughed. Oh, we've done away with that, just wear what's comfortable. But then a second later she added, When you find out where you're going, ask if you'll need a sweater.

Camp was six weeks long. The first half was psychological—everyone had to participate. The second half was arms training, familiarizing themselves with the weapons their country had purchased that year.

[8×10]

As for physical training, that had been discontinued. If they had been told one thing over and over, it was that you do not have to be an athlete to ride around in a helicopter all day. Most quadriplegics can operate a keyboard. Even a six-year-old knows what the space bar means.

An hour before shipping out he was told that there were eight places he could be sent to, but it was likely he would go north, for further training. His psych tests had him rated in the ninety-fifth percentile, and north was where they sent people like him. North for two months, then no one knows— because those who went north were never heard from again.

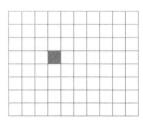

They were never married, but at one point it was necessary for them to appear that way, so they lied, and it stuck.

Now she was tired and wanted out.

When they emigrated she believed they were leaving a violent place for a safer one. It was not long before she realized safer places were unpredictable, and that violence in a safer place is the most senseless kind there is.

Like what happened to her husband.

He was on his way home from the store when suddenly he was surrounded by teenagers. They asked for his cigarettes, he shared them. After that, his money, so he emptied his pockets. Then they stopped asking and jumped on his back until it broke.

Because the crime took place under a faulty street light, the city was liable. With money from his settlement they purchased a small section of land and built a modest house. The rest they invested.

And they invested well, earning more than enough to live on, forever. But rather than continue with stocks and bonds she wanted to do something different, something fun.

So she opened an art gallery, a business she was familiar with, having volunteered at a museum back home—the same museum on whose steps her husband spent his weekends, drawing portraits of tourists to put himself through medical school. It was her hope that a gallery might revive that talent, for he could render, quite accurately, whatever was put before him.

One of the first artists she showed was a woman from a town not far from the one she grew up in. Although impressed by her intellect, she was not fond of her paintings. She liked representational work, portraits done in soft, careful strokes. But the artist preferred a harder edge, eschewing brushes for masking tape, rollers and squeegees, materials one might find at a hardware store.

When asked why she painted grids, the artist replied, I paint what I think, not what I feel. She nodded knowingly, for she had heard answers like that before. Then she asked the artist if she felt obliged to paint the world around her. At this the artist scoffed. Painting is not about obligations, it's about painting. Let the photographers take the pictures.

Despite their differences, the two became friends. They would shop together, have lunch, go swimming. She saw in the artist a model, a way to behave in a world she was not comfortable in. She was not sure what the artist saw in her, and for the longest time it did not matter.

Recently, while on a visit to the artist's studio, she noticed a sketchbook opened to a page of hastily drawn street scenes. She was intrigued by the drawings, not because they were figurative but because they reminded her of home. She asked the artist where they came from, and the artist shrugged. From my head, I guess.

She wanted to see more, but the artist told her they were not for exhibition. She offered to commission a series, for her own enjoyment, and the artist said she would think about it. A second attempt to raise the topic was met with silence.

At dinner she told her husband.

You're a romantic, he said, cutting into his steak.

[8×10]

All I'm saying is, Wouldn't it be nice to have some drawings of home?

I thought we agreed to put the past behind us.

She began to cry.

He took his napkin and wiped the corners of his mouth. It's a wonder you two are friends. You have nothing in common.

We have lots in common! she protested.

He took a sip of water, then began again. Look, he said firmly, she makes paintings you don't like. You sell one, she blames you for the ones that don't sell. She's arrogant, you're shy. If the sky is blue, she says its azure, or cerulean . . .

She left the table before he could finish.

Leave him, said the artist. Let someone else be his wife.

You don't understand.

I understand just fine. It's over, you've done your duty, let it go.

It's not that simple. I want to leave, but . . .

But what!

I can't. Not until it's okay.

What, you need permission? I'm telling you—it's okay!

That's not how it's done where I come from.

What do you mean, where you come from? Last I heard we come from the same place. When people don't get along, they part.

We do things differently.

We? said the artist. Who's we?

She turned away.

The artist stared at her. Then, quite suddenly, she grabbed a handful of blanket and gave it a yank.

Naked, she recoiled. I told you to stop doing that!

The artist straddled her, pinning her arms above her head. Look at me, she said firmly. Look at me and tell me what I want.

[8×10]

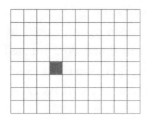

Whenever it got too wet, or he wanted to fix again, afraid his mind had wandered, he would say, Fuck it, get in his car and drive south until it stopped.

There was a woman he would visit, someone he met after he gave up trains. She was sweet, had two kids, and two more she inherited when her sister ran off with her boyfriend.

She never talked about what she did for a living, though one night, while drinking, she told him it had something to do with motels. Eight to ten clients, once or twice a week. Not all at once, of course; she was not like that. But eight to ten once or twice multiplied by whatever she was charging was a good week. Better than what the government paid her to feed and clothe four kids.

She liked her job, and because she was the only one doing it, she could be picky.

Every summer she dropped the kids at a nearby kennel, where they helped the couple running it. They were old; him in a wheelchair, her half-cracked. She took them there by cab, which she made her clients pay for, adding the receipt to her overhead. Something he would have done if he were in her shoes.

Which he was once, in her shoes.

She had big feet, big enough that when he tried her clogs on, he did not have to take his off. Not that he had small feet—but still! It was her width that impressed him. With width like that you could fit a size-ten foot into a size-eight shoe no problem.

[71]

He was never sure why that was, how a longer, thinner foot fits a shorter, wider shoe, it just does.

When he was a boy his mother told him the size of a woman's foot was relative to her birth canal. Wide foot, wide berth. This became something of an obsession with him.

During high school he met a girl with really big feet. She worked at a driving range, and it took a month before she agreed to date him. They were halfway through their third (a visit to a mine shaft, where couples tossed coins) when she said, We can do it if you want. To which he replied, Sure, like it was nothing.

There were more dates like this, and his mother was right every time.

Eventually he grew bored, leaving home for the highway. Hitchhiking, working odd jobs, turning the odd trick. After a couple of months he met a brakeman who told him he could travel longer and harder if he learned to jump trains.

He gave him some tips—where to hop on, when to hop off—and he was hooked. For the next three years that was all he did.

The trains were usually empty when he boarded them. Only once was there a woman. She was asleep, so out of respect he sat as far from her as possible. He tried to make himself small, so when she woke up she would not feel overwhelmed.

But when she did wake up, it was he who was sleeping.

It was the smell of food that woke him. He had not eaten in days. Before her was a slab of cheese and a big red apple, which she was cutting into sections, making sure he saw the knife. She offered him a piece, and he took it.

He was familiar with her T-shirt. As it turned out, they had lots in common. Same people, similar interests.

Soon they were sitting side by side, staring out the open door. Farm, factory, farm, farm . . . Like watching a movie, she said, except the door's the wrong size. He agreed. Movie screens were wider.

She mentioned where she was headed, and that she had access to an apartment. Just before jumping she asked if he wanted to join her. She knew how they could make some quick money.

A couple of hours later they were stumbling out of a bar. Her hand brushed against his, and he grabbed it. She pushed him away, told him exactly what she thought of him, and he was excited to be spoken to so firmly.

They bought a six-pack, opened a can and passed it back and forth between them. They took big loud sips whenever somebody looked their way. It was raining, but they were oblivious. Laughing, tripping over each other, her more than him.

Once in the apartment, he threw her on the bed. One of the cans sprang loose and fell against the radiator, a thin white spray shooting up.

Man down! he cried, scooping up the can, and her cackle filled the room.

She took off everything but her black knee socks. He reached for them, but she pushed him away.

Hey, what's up with the socks? How come you're keeping your socks on?

I'm cold, she said, pulling him towards her.

Ten seconds later he was out.

He awoke twice. The first time she was straddling him, rocking back and forth like a bell; the second time beside him, braiding her hair. She was talking about her childhood, how she grew up next to railroad tracks. A few muffled words, then something about an accident, how she learned to put her feet on before most kids tied their shoes.

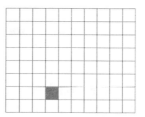

She liked rough men. She liked the way they moved, the way they crashed into things. You can always tell what you're getting, she would tell her employees. And they would laugh.

Not with her, of course.

But she knew the difference. Just as she knew that when people laugh at something, you learn more about the laughers than what they thought was funny. Because people laugh at things that are not funny. Or if they are funny, their laugh is usually disproportionate to the humour that got them laughing in the first place.

She could tell when someone laughed too hard, or for too long. She could always spot a faker.

Like many in her field, she grew up in the business. Unlike most, she eschewed the family model and, as soon as she was old enough, went to work for others, before going it alone.

The first years were difficult. But eventually she got the hang of it. It helped having employees whose knowledge she could draw on. She learned from them many lessons, one of which was to set herself up to be laughed at.

Like her set piece on rough men.

I once knew a man who was so rough, she would begin, and her employees would drone back, How rough was he? Then the punchline.

Even before launching into her jokes she knew what the response would be. Not the words, but the delivery. In that respect, her employees were more like performers than droners, even though their youth—and the resentment that often goes with it—gave them good reason.

Eventually she learned that her employees' performances served as a buffer, a mask. Pretending to feel what they were feeling was their way of maintaining self-respect.

One day she stopped short of the punchline, letting her joke hang there like a wet rag. It was a good ten seconds before one of them let out a snort, and the rest followed. So what was funny—what got the laugh—was not what was said but the pause, the omission.

It was a nervous laugh, but a sincere one. It had everything to do with what her employees found uncomfortable. Which was just as well, she thought, because that was her product: discomfort, and its uses.

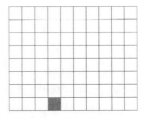

He was up early, her big dog scratching at the door.

He was doing the dishes when she came up behind him, wrapping her arms around his waist. You don't have to do those, she whispered.

I know, he whispered back, I want to.

She hooked her thumbs into his belt loops. Wouldn't you rather be in bed with me than washing those fucking dishes?

Let me tidy up first, make it nice for your mom.

Fuck my mom, she said.

Fuck your mom? No thanks. He rinsed a plate and filed it in the drying rack.

On her toes this time, her mouth at his ear, I want you. I want your balls against my ass.

One more plate, he said.

She pushed off. She won't notice, she's fucking out of it!

It was just noise now. A truck passing, a canvas tent being torn in half. She was upset. You like me, right? You're not using me to get to my mom, are you?

Yes and no, he assured her. Now c'mon, be a pal, get me those cups by the bed.

Her feet like seal fins, slapping at the lino. Under the suds, a reef of silverware.

She returned with a single cup, plopping it in the sink. You're tense, let me rub your neck. She took hold of his shoulders, rubbing until her hands got bored and slithered under the waistband of his jeans. I'm never sure how guys arrange themselves down there.

He picked at a piece of egg stuck to a steak knife.

She took hold of his penis, gave it a squeeze. It's sad how something so beautiful has to spend its life in the dark.

He could feel himself stiffen. You shouldn't talk about your mom like that, it's not nice.

I know, she whispered. So c'mon—let's go.

He followed after her, stepping over her housecoat, hopping out of his pants. She knelt on the bed and lifted her ass, the soles of her feet a dusty grey. The floor would need sweeping too, he thought.

He squatted behind her, gave his penis a couple of jerks

before pressing it against her crack. She reached underneath and took his balls, rolling them over her clitoris—her lips wet, her breath heavy.

I want you inside me, she whispered.

He complied, though he knew her mother would be arriving any minute. She would need help up the stairs. Halfway in he withdrew. His cock glistened, the head flared.

Don't stop, she said, and he repeated his actions until they took on a life of their own.

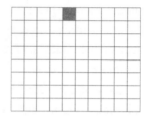

Their orders were to patrol the marsh at the northern edge of the city. A former bird sanctuary, where the enemy, according to one source, had been spotted.

But after three weeks, nothing. Not even a bird. Try telling that to command, he would mutter to himself, one drenched foot after another.

Four times a night they climbed a hill, checking on a cluster of homes, all of them blown out, abandoned. It was during their last visit, just as the sun was rising, that one of his men noticed a figure moving towards a stand of trees.

Get down, he motioned.

Lifting his binoculars, he saw that it was not a person but a dog—and it seemed to be favouring its right front paw. Three of his men chased after it.

They were fifty feet from the trees when suddenly a fountain of dirt, the man in front exploding in five directions. A beat later, two more explosions. But these were smaller, more compact.

[8×10]

One man rolled on the ground, his hands between his legs; the other just stood there, grinning, his pants blown off—the same pair he had mended for him only hours before.

Don't move! he called out, and the man without pants looked incredulous. He took two steps forward, and another fountain.

Back at command he was told that the mines had been planted a month ago, and why had it taken him so long? He replied that his orders were to patrol the marsh, and that the mines were off the grid.

As the debriefing dragged on, it dawned on him that the emphasis was no longer on what happened but what should have happened. They began to question his initiative, his desire to lead; they felt he was distracted. He knew then that he would never make promotion.

The more they asked, the less he had to say. Eventually he stopped talking altogether. He just stood there, and took it.

When they were ready his superiors stopped too. For the longest time it was just the two parties staring at each other, dispassionately, as if the other were holding out.

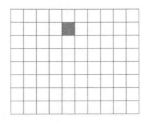

And so, she said yawning, when she awoke—when the princess awoke—she returned to the castle and the two lived happily ever after.

She closed the book and tucked it behind the headboard, careful not to wake her daughter. She was about to stand when the girl's eyes flipped open, startling her.

Which two? asked the girl.

The prince and princess, said the mother, her heart racing. The prince and the princess lived—

Why not the princess and the other princess? asked the girl. I liked her.

No you didn't. Two people can't live together if one of them is evil.

She's prettier.

You only imagine her to be prettier, said the mother, pulling up the covers. Besides, it's what's inside that counts.

Her daughter closed her eyes, squinching them.

To herself she counted one, two, three—

What's evil again? asked the daughter, her eyes still squinched.

Evil is where you don't care about others, you only care about—

The prince is evil! the girl declared.

The prince and princess love each other very much.

No response.

Four, five, six—

Is my father—?

Ah, remember what we talked about?

The girl yawned, rolled over, taking the covers with her.

Seven, eight, nine . . .

The sky was pink and fading fast. She tilted the jug off the counter, steadying it with her knee as she filled her cup. Not a drop spilled. Good, she said to herself, improvement.

She grabbed her tobacco and stepped onto the deck, the boards still warm beneath her feet. She lowered herself onto the swing, bringing her legs up beside her, where they curled like dogs.

In her notebook she wrote:

> Summer found its way into everything. From the sage sprouting through the rotten porch to the nails that held it together.

She crossed out *it*, thought a minute, then replaced it with a new *it*.

Then she crossed it out again.

After refilling her cup she returned to the swing, rolled a cigarette, then pressed her big toe against a nailhead, absorbing its heat. Its energy gone, she wrote:

Rust, sage, tobacco. Everything had that just-
baked smell.

She crossed that out too, and below it wrote:

It was just the two of them now; he wasn't
coming back.

Just as well, she muttered, he would've found out sooner
or later; somebody would've told him.

Not that it mattered. Why should it matter if their kid
wasn't his? Especially now, after all these years. And especially after telling her how much he loved them.

How do you unlove someone? she wondered. Unless you
never loved them in the first place, that's how! She thought
about writing this down.

She flicked her cigarette over the railing, blowing
after it a purple cone of smoke. Lucky for us he found out
when he did. She took a sip. Any longer and who knows?
Another sip.

The view from her porch was of seven tree-lined ridges
winding their way down to a silver strip of water. But not
at the moment. All that was out there now was night. Hard
black night.

She liked it like that, knowing what was out there but
not having to see it.

Night, she wrote. A great black curtain/ she could open/
and close/ with her eyes

Her cigarette had ignited something. She picked up her

lantern and stumbled towards it, dousing it with the contents of her cup.

Back on the swing, she reached for her notebook. Lucky for us, she began.

[8×10]

She was on her lunch break when she saw him. He was leaning against the jewellery counter—the man from the boat over, the one who stole her necklace.

It was not an expensive necklace—a thin metal chain looped through a black plastic square. But because it belonged to her grandmother, it had value.

It's not worth anything, please, give it back.

But he kept it anyway.

As the journey wore on, she would approach him, plead with him, Why can't I have my necklace? For the longest time he denied taking it—until she caught him moving it from one pocket to another. If it bothers you so much, why don't you tell your husband? and he would laugh. That shut her up.

He was looking at watches. The clerk had taken three from the display case. But the clerk did not trust him either. She kept her hands close by.

They were children's watches, done up in happy reds and yellows. As she moved closer she noticed their faces were decorated with cartoon characters. Each had one arm shorter than the other. Not unlike him, she thought, though in his case, it was his leg, not his arm, that was shorter.

A week before landing, he had begun to pester her, telling her she could have her necklace back if she put her mouth here, and he would point. No, she told him. And if her husband ever found out . . . At which point he would laugh and walk away.

He pointed to the pink watch. How much? The clerk told him. He pushed off, disgusted. The clerk shrugged; it was not her place to haggle. She reached for the watches, but he grabbed her wrist. I'll take it, but I'm not paying the tax.

Before the clerk could answer, she called out, Then who will pay for your shoe?

He turned sharply.

She was pointing at his foot, the one with the modified sole. He did not recognize her. Or if he did, he denied her that too.

What does my shoe have to do with it? he said.

The government collects taxes to support cripples like you. Why should you be exempt?

Enraged, he picked up a watch and threw it at her. Then he picked up another, this time hitting her in the ear. It hurt, but the pain felt good. There were witnesses.

He was about to throw a third when security grabbed him and wrestled him to the ground. See that man? she said to the gathering crowd. Take a good look. He is a rapist. He raped my husband, and after that he tried to rape me too.

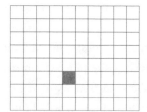

[8×10]

His record collection covered the entire wall. He asked her to put something on, and she pulled out the first thing.

The sleeve was black, the disc inside unlabelled. Eight tracks on one side, ten on the other. She put on the side with ten tracks and lowered the needle. Although the record looked new, all she could hear were scratches. What is this? she asked.

Ice? he called out.

Sure, she said, lifting the needle, lining it up with the second track.

Same thing.

He handed her her drink, thanking her again for returning his satchel.

What are we listing to? she asked.

The sound of old records.

Why?

A record of activity. The sound of wear. He gestured towards the couch.

Do you listen to it much? she said, taking a seat.

This is the first time.

Can you imagine why anyone would listen to a record like this?

Sure, he said, turning up the volume, it's a sound we don't hear much any more, but years ago it was the first thing you heard when the needle dropped.

The sound of something falling?

He smiled, took a sip.

She looked back at the turntable, then added, Or a record of something falling.

Even better, he said, reaching for his satchel.

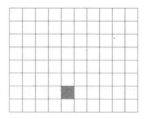

The tires on her bike were flat. It scared her that both tires could go flat at the same time, especially when they had been filled the day before. Scarier still, that she rode three blocks without noticing.

She had been scared a lot lately, though she was not sure why. Not knowing only compounded her fear.

What was she afraid of? The neighbourhood?

True, it had changed. The children had grown, moved on. Followed by their parents, who sold their homes to people she would never meet, investors who rented to a new kind of family—those who had drugs, not blood, in common.

But these were not the aggressive, in-your-face type drugs she read about—these were comforting drugs, working drugs, drugs that behaved like long underwear on the coldest day of the year, or a glass of water on the hottest.

[8×10]
She felt safe among these people, most of whom were younger. Artists, students, activists. She could hear them from her bicycle. Not their voices but their music, which was slow and plodding. Hardly the kind of music she listened to, though she was never one to judge. Sometimes she found it soothing.

But that would change too. As fast as her tires went flat, the music would grow louder—until one day she would find it inside her, on the off-beat, pulsing. She would pedal home as fast as she could, swallowing pills from a hand that shook so violently she would think it belonged to someone else.

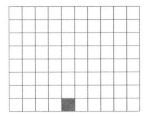

When her name was announced, the audience erupted. She picked up her guitar, took a deep breath and stepped from the wings. As she came into view, the crowd grew louder.

Sidling up to the microphone, she asked, How's every-body doin' out there?

Louder.

She cast her eyes about the hall. She could see the first two rows, and the lights above, but beyond that everything was black.

I'm gonna sing a song for you, a song that began in a place most of us start out in and, in some cases, return to; where words are few and infinitely reusable, until bigger words come along and put an end to how we think about our feelings. And in offering this song to you I'd like to ded-icate it to someone we're all familiar with—a singer, a song-writer, someone we love and admire. She looked to her left, to the man who had introduced her. Maybe if you clap loud enough, he'll join in.

Applause.

She waited a beat before strumming a one-five chord pattern. 1-2-3-1-2-3-4-5-6-1-2-3-1-2-3-4-5-6. When the words came out, they looked like this:

> Oh where do we go
> Up or down or in or
> Out into the street
> Where do we go
> Now that things have gone full
> Circle in the air
> Maybe it's over
> If it is I want to
> Ask you once again

Where do we go
And if you are going
Can I go with you

Oooo what do we do
Sit around and kiss and
Tell it like it is
What do we do
Find ourselves a job and
Work it out at night
Maybe it's over
If it is I want to
Ask you once again
Where do we go
And if you are going
Can I go with you

So what do we know
Years go by and still we
Think about these things
What do we know
I know I will always
Love you with my life
Maybe it's over
If it is I want to
Ask you once again
Where do we go
And if you are going
Can I go with you

Only you
Only you

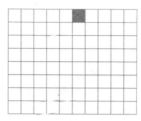

A grinding of gears from the service road dividing his wife's grave from the crematorium. He did not have to look to know it was the bus from the old folks' home. He glanced at his watch: he had been kneeling for over an hour, though to him it felt like seconds.

He remembered when his wife took the bus to work, when she was still on days, how the route had become so familiar to her that she no longer noticed the sights along the way. It was in response to his question about a tower under construction that she told him how the building seemed in a constant state of near completion. It was then that he realized she was no longer going to work but spending her days elsewhere. There never was a tower on that route.

The flowers in his hands were tightly bound; water from the stems made the knot impossible. He picked at the string with his thumbnail, at the same time recalling the girl who put them together, her cheerfulness, her love of bunches. He could have sworn it was a bow she had tied.

Eventually he gave up. Opening his penknife, he cut the string and dropped the flowers one by one into the cup by his wife's marker. He had a few left over, so he laid them on a grave near the entrance. An older grave, one of the first in the cemetery. It bore the same name as his son.

[8×10]

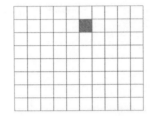

War had changed him, he kept telling himself.

But he only half listened.

War had changed everything.

Who was he before shipping out? The question came up during his sponge bath. Not what the orderly was saying but the rhythm of his touch. Like code, he thought. The question tapped into him.

Would it have made a difference had he not gone to war on his twenty-first birthday, that the first thing he did, as a man, was shoot a boy in the face?

Who was he before shipping out?

He awoke on his back. With effort, he was able to lift himself onto his elbows. A rectangular ward, white, with bits of red mixed in. Blood, crosses, poppies, lipstick.

Over a hundred beds, all of them occupied. Most of the patients were comatose, though some hovered in between, their moans like old machines. He shut his eyes. The room seemed to float. A parachute of anguish and pain.

An orderly came on shift. He watched as the man moved from bed to supply room to bed again. Not once was he given instruction. Like a robot, he thought.

He drifted off again, this time dreaming of a picnic basket, a checkered blanket and the blue sky above.

The soldier next to him had lost his legs. He kept telling people how it was the best thing that happened to him. Like money in the bank, he kept saying (through gritted teeth).

When he was able to sit, they put him in a wheelchair and pushed him to the garden. There, he met a soldier with similar injuries, a fellow insubordinate. She had an endless supply of cigarettes, which had something to do with her working in stores. Both of them were lucky—they would keep their legs.

She told him the story of a comatose soldier who became pregnant during her convalescence. This was not uncommon. Comatose soldiers were a source of comfort. But in this soldier's case, penetration was impossible given the nature of her injuries.

After much probing it was determined that her pregnancy was related to the bullet that felled her. During a raid her commanding officer, who later died, was found to have had a bullet pass through his scrotum. The bullet was the carrier. Tests backed this up.

She regained consciousness during her second trimester. When told of her pregnancy she said she was not surprised. In fact, she claims to have dreamt it.

A general caught wind of her story and had her moved to a room of her own. Miracles are good for morale! he announced. A few days later, she miscarried.

On her way back to the ward, a reporter caught up with her, asked how she was feeling. Relieved, was her reply. When asked why, she said she could not bear to have a child born of conflict. When reminded that the child would not have been born of conflict so much as conceived by it (a miracle!), she turned to the camera and said, That's just the kind of hair-splitting that got us into this war in the first place.

[8×10]

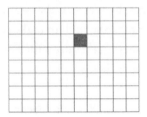

The assignment was familiar enough. But this time they were supplying the means.

Usually he brought his own tools. He preferred it that way. Unless he was plugging into something already in motion.

He was blindfolded and put in the back of a leather-upholstered car. He could hear his contact breathing beside him. You're well? the contact asked, if for no other reason than to announce his presence. He nodded.

You've come a long way, said a voice in front. Last we met, you were raiding people's medicine cabinets.

It was then that he knew who he was dealing with.

They drove to what smelled like a slaughterhouse. Once inside, he was introduced to a man whose accent he could not place. The man took him by the arm and led him deeper into the building.

When the blindfold came off, he was standing in a room full of electronic equipment. On a table, supported by an armature, a telescopic rifle wired to a small metal box. Built into the box was an electronic screen, and below that, a toggle switch.

He was approached by a man in a light grey lab coat. Ever seen a weapon like this before?

He had not.

It's quite simple, really. As you can see, the gun is attached to a stand, which is placed on a flat, stable surface. As flat and as stable as possible. He looked at him.

He nodded.

The man picked up the box and took hold of the switch. Rotate the switch until the crosshairs intersect. He pulled the switch towards him, and the barrel of the gun rose slowly.

He glanced at the screen. The crosshairs had aligned over an apple at the far end of the room.

Where's the trigger? he asked.

The man turned the box over and pushed aside a small shutter, revealing a tiny hole. Taking a ballpoint pen from his pocket, he pressed the tip into the hole, and the gun emitted a red laser. Press it again, he said, and you have your projectile. Here, he said, handing over the box—you try.

He took the pen and pressed it into the hole. The apple exploded.

How much does it weigh?

Why?

It looks heavy. I might need help.

You won't, said a voice behind him.

He recognized the accent. Without turning, he asked, So what's the deal?

We give you a time and a place and a photo. You show up, identify the target, take it out. When you're finished, detach the box. You'll have ninety seconds before the weapon self-destructs.

How soon do you want this done?

A week, maybe later.

How much later?

Could be six months, could be a year.

A year!

Footsteps.

It was his contact. He straightened up. But instead of a blindfold, a pillowcase.

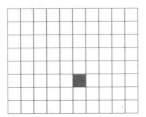

All he had to do was pull the trigger. The others would grab him, bend him over. All he had to do was keep him in the bar until closing time, then, after everyone had left, walk him outside, pull out the gun, point it, and pull the trigger. Then he was free. And for what? Didn't even have to look at the guy. Just follow along, and when the others grabbed him, pull out the gun, touch it to the back of his neck, poof. Simple. And if he had never handled a gun before, they would show him how. How to clean it, how to load it, how to cock it. Easy. So easy a child could do it. And if he had a problem with that, remember, it's social work. Because this guy is scum, right? The lowest of the low. So it was up to him to get this piece of puke off the street. Because who wants to live in a world with shit like that running around? Who wants to see families uprooted, kids put in foster care? Think of it as social work, keeping good families together. Families who show respect. As for scum—and here is another thing about scum—they don't have families. And if they do, if for some fluke reason they do, they abuse them. They must. Because they're greedy, only in it for themselves. So yeah, all he had to do was pull the trigger and those kids over there—see those kids, laughing and playing? No, really, look at them. Look at those kids. It's because of him that kids like that will have parents to go home to. Loving parents. And what better feeling is that, to have a father and a mother who hug you and kiss you and cook you hot meals? What could be better than that! All for pulling a trigger. One lousy trigger. If only life were that simple. If only everything was like that.

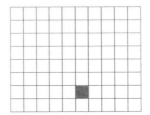

[8×10]

It had been thirty seconds since she last looked out. She parted the curtains. A white van, and someone behind a tree, smoking. She could see a cigarette, pulsing.

She knew why they were there. But were they waiting for her, or just watching?

She had done something wrong, that she knew. But no one would tell her what exactly. He is upset with you. You have pissed him off royally. But when she asked for details, they just stared back at her, incredulous, as if it was their turn to take offence.

Her first impulse was to run. But that would only complicate things. Not doing anything made her anxious. They had trained her to be decisive, but what do you do when you do not know what you have done?

After much hand-wringing, she chose to stay put, await instruction. She stocked up on groceries, bought a deadbolt for the basement door, distributed weapons throughout the house.

The following day the van pulled up.

And now, a day later, it was still there.

She went to her closet, took out her binoculars. The headlights from an oncoming car would light up the van's interior. Knowing what these people looked like would give her insight into their intentions.

A minute passed. No cars.

Another minute. Same.

She had been pressing the binoculars hard against her face, and her eyes began to hurt. She lowered the binoculars—when something shifted in the dormer across the street. What had always been a soft rectangle of light was suddenly a chaos of shadows.

Someone was leaning over, rummaging through a box. She tweaked the focus ring. It was not the woman who lived there, but someone younger, quicker. A thief?

There was a knock at her door.

She froze.

Now they were pounding.

She made her way downstairs, stopping on the landing to take a peek: a woman in a dressing gown, a cigarette dangling from her lips—the woman from across the street! She seemed distressed, and kept looking over her shoulder.

Instinctively she ran to the door. But when she opened it, the woman was gone. She poked her head out—the van was gone too. She looked up at the dormer and saw a flash.

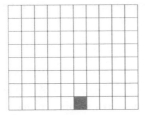

[8×10] As soon as his name was announced, the audience erupted. He took a breath, stepped from the wings and made his way towards the mike.

A surge of applause.

He waved, removed a pick from his pocket and gave his guitar a quick, hard strum. The chord blew back from the monitor, hitting him in the chest. Thank you for coming, he said.

The audience roared.

Another chord, but this time he let it mingle with the whoops and whistles. He looked up, into the spotlight, and sang:

> Cryin', cryin'
> Cryin' every night for you
> Starin' at my picture tube
> I love the way you sing the news
> Every night on channel two
> Cryin', cryin'
> Cryin' every night for you
> And every place you take me to

Do do do do do-do do
Do do do do do-do do
Doo-dle-oot-do doodle-oodle-oot-do
Do do do do do-do do
Do do do do do-do do

Lyin', lyin'
Lyin' every night to me
From a desk I cannot see
If you are public property
How come you're so mean to me?
Lyin', lyin'
Lyin' every night to me
Look at the world, what do you see?

The girl of my dreams is on TV.

Do do do do do-do do
Do do do do do-do do
Doo-dle-oot-do doodle-oodle-oot-do
Do do do do do-do do
Do do do do do-do do

Another sixteen bars and he was done.

He ripped through three more before checking his tuning,
impressing the audience with his knowledge of local affairs,
careful not to appear too partisan.

Not that his politics were ambiguous. Indeed, what his
fans cared about, what attracted them, had less to do with

what he said than how he said it, as if, at the end of the day, poetry and passion, not ideology and rhetoric, would prevail.

When it appeared he was about to sing another, he announced that now might be a good time to say a few words about someone near and dear to him, and that if everyone put their hands together, maybe this person might come out and sing a few words of her own.

[8×10] He did not have to say her name for the audience to know who he was talking about. But he said it anyway. And when he did, they went nuts.

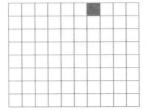

It was a difficult assignment. Kidnap the daughter of a local businessman, cut off her head and impale it on a fence post outside her father's girlfriend's home. Easy enough, but he only had forty-eight hours to do it.

The girl was under constant surveillance. Not a bodyguard—she made a sport of ditching them—but a car that followed her every move.

Once a week she went ice-skating with a boy from her physics class. As luck would have it, their skating day fell within his window. The venue was also a plus. The rink was popular, and the crowd would provide him his screen. Not only that, he was familiar with the layout, having spent parts of his youth there, training.

It did not take long to identify the car. A small import, built to manoeuvre. Inside were three men, two in suits and a runner in back. It was a common configuration, the runner deployed in situations where cars were either prohibited or impractical.

And he looked like a runner too. Dressed in a track suit and trainers, a pouch around his waist filled with communications devices, weapons. The runner would patrol the stands while the suits waited outside in the car.

At least that was what he thought. For no sooner had he arrived when he noticed the runner lacing up his skates. This would also work in his favour: once he had the girl, the runner would need at least a minute to get into his shoes. And a minute was as good as mile as far as he was concerned.

The runner was an exceptional skater, more balletic than fast. The girl, on the other hand, was a novice, her ankles bent, her arms like windmills. Her friend was no better.

Yet another plus. Poor skaters generally stayed near the boards. And that was where he would wait, twenty feet from the exit where the cleaner dumped its ice. All he had to do was reach out and grab her.

Which he did, the runner on the opposite side of the rink. Even in protest she helped his cause: kicking her friend in the throat, severing his jugular. The perfect distraction.

A few short hops and he was at the exit. However, after opening the door, who should he see getting out of their car but the suits.

Thinking quickly, he dragged the girl back into the building, taking refuge behind the ice cleaner.

The suits burst in, the taller one first. Coming the other way, the runner, still in his skates.

Instead of searching the building, the taller suit lays into the runner. The fuck you think you're doing? The runner, more embarrassed than apologetic, started to undo his laces, at which point the smaller suit pulls out a gun and shoots him in the back of the head, tossing his weapon behind the ice cleaner as he and his partner race for the door.

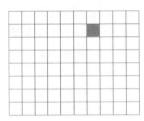

She noticed it before her daughter. Not her belly but her behaviour—the fatigue, the vomiting. How could she know what was happening to her? How could she know if she had never been told?

I don't feel well.

I know. Lie down, I'll make soup.

A moment later. Why don't I feel well?

She asked his name, the daughter told her. Hearing it made her eye twitch. (It could have been any name.) Did her daughter notice her eye twitch? And if so, was she thinking,

Does my mother know her eye twitched? Does she know that I noticed?

We didn't do anything, we just danced, is all. When pressed, she elaborated. We went for a walk, but we didn't, you know . . .

Her daughter was no liar. Which is not to say she knew what the truth was either, though she always told it.

When her daughter was born she decided she would deal with her mistakes the moment she made them. Let context supply her her blackboard and chalk. Yet if someone told her her daughter's first mistake would be getting pregnant, she would have thought them extreme. Birth to pregnancy—what about all those baby steps in between?

She remembered little of her own childhood. Had she been caught in a lie? Not a lie so much as its consequences.

She was eight. After her father died, her mother moved them to a smaller house. There was a girl across the lane, pretty, around her age. One day the girl peeked over the fence. Do you want to go swimming? My mom will take us. She wanted to, but pride tugged at her. I can't, she replied, it's my birthday. My mother and I are making doll clothes.

Later, while doing the dishes, she heard a knock at the door. Her mother was in the next room, drunk. She did her best to head her off.

It was the girl from across the lane. Her hair was wet, and she smelled of shampoo. Happy birthday, she said, holding out a long white box wrapped in red ribbon. Her mother glared at the girl. Who are you trying to kid! and the girl burst into tears.

The next morning she found her mother passed out at the kitchen table. Beside her, a doll, its dress ripped to shreds.

Do you like him?

Her daughter shrugged.

She regretted the juxtaposition. What she meant to ask— what she wanted to know—concerned his character. Was he responsible? Had she met his family? She was digging, and her daughter knew it. Do you love him?

He's a soldier.

Did he make any promises?

I don't know.

Will you see him again?

She looked away.

Did he say when he'd be back?

Stop torturing me!

So he's left you then. She looked at her stomach. Both of you.

She was crying. Not bawling, just sniffles. Only when her daughter broke down did she reach for her and draw her close.

[8×10]

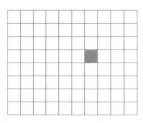

His surgeon told him he might never walk again. He asked for details. The surgeon nodded.

Although his spinal cord had not been severed, it had undergone enough trauma that he would be in pain the rest of his life. Not the dull recurring pain of a sore back, but a pain so wretched, so relentless, that the medication required to numb it would prevent him from holding a thought for more than a couple of seconds. As the surgeon saw it, his best chance at a normal life was to cut the cord.

It took him a moment to gather his thoughts. In saying that I might never walk again, are you saying I'll give in to the pain?

It is likely.

Are there no alternatives?

None surgical.

What about non-surgical?

None that I'm aware of.

He noticed the surgeon had a mole over his left eye. In time it would grow meaty, sprout hairs. Who would I talk to about this?

The surgeon shrugged. I can't recommend anyone.

I'm not interested in anyone, he said firmly, I'm interested in someone with knowledge of spinal cord injuries—who isn't a surgeon!

The surgeon checked his watch. We'll continue with morphine, but in decreasing doses. We can't keep you on it forever, of course. Once we determine your threshold, we'll take it from there.

I feel fine, he said.

The doctor smiled, put his pen in his pocket.

I'm not kidding! he shouted after him. I can even feel my toes!

That night he dreamt of his injury. Not the incident—those kids who jumped him—but what it looked like from the inside.

He lived in a tower thirty-three storeys high. Although his apartment was third from the top, its height did not translate into a better view. Nor was it spacious. In fact, the highest suites were also the smallest. But no one knew this, not even him. Occupants rarely spoke to each other (apart from the work they had in common). An outside view was impossible. No one left the building.

From his window, he saw what everyone else saw. Not a sky but a jungle of muscle, ligaments and vessels. This was their world. A world of texture and tension, rendered in reds, whites and blues. A vertical world where all that mattered was gravity.

His mail had just been pushed through the slot when suddenly he felt a jolt. He kept his balance, but there was a second one, more violent than the first. A series of smaller jolts followed as he crawled to the window.

It was raining. Great gobs of blood, with some clear stuff mixed in. In the distance, a piece of lung, billowing. It reminded him of what his curtains did at night, when the temperature dropped.

Whatever rocked the building had impacted the suites below. Nerves were down, snapping like whips. After each crack, a shriek, then the hiss of something burning.

[8×10]

Yet as bad as it seemed, the building felt secure. The problem, as far as he could tell, was the rain—it was gathering at the bottom, and people were drowning. He could hear their shouts, and a voice over the intercom, ordering everyone to relax, stay put.

Which he did, initially. But the rising temperature, coupled with concern for those below, had a suffocating effect. So he left the apartment to check on his neighbours. To his surprise, the elevator was in working order.

In the hours that followed he made several trips up and down the building—calming the children, assisting the old and infirm. But it was those in between who were most at risk.

Indeed, those who at first appeared in shock were coming out of their stupors with an aggression that seemed as odd to them as it did to him. Incredulous warriors, lashing out at anyone who stood in their way. When he tried to intervene they turned on him, attacking with such ferociousness that he had no choice but to step aside.

Until he could stand it no longer.

A child was being swarmed, so he stepped in, and took a beating so severe he thought it might never end.

He awoke in his apartment. A vaporous figure would visit at intervals, feeding him soup through a straw. He liked what he was drinking, and felt better. However, after a few feedings he realized that the soup was not meant to cure him but to keep him there, inactive.

He opened his eyes. A nurse's face. She smiled, asked him how he was doing. Before he could answer she stuck a thermometer in his mouth. He blinked, and the next thing he saw was his surgeon.

I asked you how you were feeling, he said.

He had to think for a second. I don't know. Same as yesterday, I guess.

Mock incredulity. Yesterday you were in agony!

He felt nauseous. What day is it?

[8×10] If I told you, you might think it was the day after the last time we spoke.

Try me.

It's been a week, said the surgeon, glancing at his legs.

It was then that he knew what was coming.

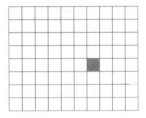

He took milk in his coffee, not cream. And he always had something to eat. Half the time it was muffins; the other half, unpredictable.

When they stopped selling danishes, he was the first to notice, though he never ordered them. The following morning they were back on the shelf, and for the next seven days he had one.

Then he disappeared.

She had been working at the bakery a year. When she

was hired she was told that her evaluations would be based on service, not sales. The rest was secondary—using the tongs, folding boxes, operating the cash register. Machines could do that, automatons.

The first week took everything she had. There was so much to remember. Then, as if by magic, the job kicked in, and she could do it in her sleep. The only problem was the customers.

The regulars were awful; most wanted discounts. Some were former employees, so they knew what they could get away with. It bothered her having to put up with these people, but she endured.

She had no idea how long he had been coming. No way of knowing, either. Not without giving her workmates the right idea. If they knew, they would tease her, and teasing was how they drew you in.

That was the last thing she wanted—to be drawn in. She liked her anonymity and worked hard to keep it.

He was not particularly attractive, nor did he have any tics or idiosyncrasies. In some ways he was not unlike the job itself: the more she got to know him, the easier he became.

After work he would walk her home, sometimes stopping at the market where she liked to shop. They would cook together, and later he would sit at her desk and watch her draw. When the time came, she would take him to bed, tucking him in with a tenderness she was never sure of.

One night she took him with such force her pillow ripped in two. But instead of rolling over, she found herself on her knees, staring back from the closet mirror—laughing, crying, done with him for good.

[8×10]

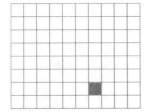

After her treatment she took what money she had left and went looking for a place to live. An ad for a farmhouse caught her eye.

The farm had been in the same family almost a hundred years, but the last version were not interested in cattle or corn so they sold it to someone who was. Someone who, despite showing up in chaps and a stetson, a great big horse between his legs, All rarin' to go, as he kept putting it, all rarin' to breed cattle and husk corn! turned out to be a fraud, a speculator who, upon taking possession, shooed the chickens, flipped the equipment and divided the land into parcels, selling most of it to developers except for a small stubborn spur where the original farmhouse stood, an area too brittle to support the kinds of projects developers were developing these days, but which suited her purposes fine.

The house was structurally sound, though little had been done to the interior. According to the agent, the family had been using it for preserves, which he brought up more than once during the half-hour drive from his office.

Didn't know what to make of them at first, he said. Looked like body parts. Some had labels. Peaches, pickles. I found a jar of plums almost fifty years old!

Fifty years old. She wondered what a plum that old might taste like. Would it make you drunk, would it kill you? What did you do with them? she asked.

He looked at her in horror. Threw them out, of course!

The house was two storeys high and faced south. Before it, a forest of rose bushes covered in morning glory. A narrow path led to the portico. Most of the cobbles had been removed. For the second house, he told her.

They were greeted by a long, wide hallway, a staircase at either end. The staircase closest to the entrance had a landing, the farthest one did not.

From his coat pocket he removed a piece of paper, and read, Upstairs: four bedrooms, thirteen by sixteen, each with closet. Between the two rooms facing south, a smaller bedroom. The first staircase leads to the first two rooms; the one at the end is for servants . . .

He continued, but by then she had tuned him out, preferring to experience the house on her own.

To the right of the hallway was a room slightly smaller than the one above it. In the middle, a cast-iron four-poster. He kicked one of the legs. Weird place for a bed, huh? Beside the front door?

Not really, she said, shifting her attention to the long wooden table in the adjoining room. Back then, you kept the infirm on the main floor, so you could tend them better.

He took hold of a bedpost and watched himself give it a shake. Yep, I was gonna chuck this with the preserves, but I might have a buyer.

She liked the bed. It suited the house. How much are you asking?

He smiled. How much will you give me?

She stepped towards the adjoining room. I might like the table as well.

[8×10]

He took out a pen and started a list.

To the left of the entrance, a longer, slightly narrower room: the parlour. It, too, had an adjoining room, though this one was smaller than the one with the table. Three of the walls were lined with shelves. In the middle of the fourth was the hearth.

The kitchen, he said of the adjoining room.

She looked at him. What makes you think it was a kitchen?

That's where I found the preserves. He pointed to the shelves. Peaches, pickles. There were plums dating back—

Those are bookshelves, she said. They were built for books.

No ma'am, he said confidently. That's where they kept the food. In the olden days you had to keep the food off the floor, else the rats would get it.

And that fireplace, she said, gesturing towards the east wall, I suppose that's where they cooked their meals?

In the olden days.

The adjoining room led to a piazza. From there, a door leading back to the hallway and the rear stairs. On the other side of the stairs, the kitchen.

Here we have the work room, he said, stepping past her. This is where the men retired after supper, to tinker, fix bridles . . .

Her attention was drawn to the room behind it: the wash room. Halfway up the wall, an outline where a sink had been attached. On the floor before it, two well-worn grooves.

Beyond the kitchen was a larger room, with vents instead of windows: the dairy. She shut her eyes and took a deep breath. She could almost smell the butter.

As you can tell from the outside, this room was added later. It's where they put the servants, once they started doing well.

Who, the servants? she asked.

No, no, no, he laughed. Farming was big business in those days. You can tell how big by the add-ons—and the size of their second houses.

She had noticed the second house on the drive over— about five times bigger than the one they were standing in. She knew a house like that could not have been built with money but many hands working together. No such thing as carpenters in those days, just neighbours, all of whom were farmers.

He swung his briefcase onto the counter, flipping open the locks. After the next phase, there's plans to turn the second house into an activities centre. He pulled out a folder. I have an artist's rendering if you'd like to see it.

The rendering reminded her of the boxes models came in. As a child she remembered overhearing a man tell his son how the contents of the box, once assembled, never added up to the drawing, and that the only thing inside a box like that was disappointment.

He returned the folder to his briefcase, then followed her back to the wash room, almost tripping over her as she crouched down to run her hand over the grooved floor.

So yeah, he continued, they'll preserve the exterior but gut the insides. They want to keep it as open as possible. He looked around. Wanted to do that here, but the walls are load-bearing.

She ignored him.

Then, as if to himself, Yep, the guy who designed this place—not the brightest bulb in the world. No foresight whatsoever.

The guy? she said, getting to her feet. What makes you think it was a guy?

[8×10]

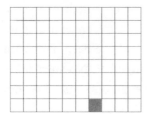

You looked great tonight, he said, gearing down for the turn.

She was staring out her window. The river glistened and she wanted to touch it. Just keep your eye on the road, she said.

Around the corner stood a farmhouse. Ahead of that, a

hill thick with trees. Traffic going up was slow, with nothing coming down. It was dusk.

He turned to her. We've done enough shows for one year. Let's go north, do some fishing.

Sit in a boat all day with you? Forget it.

We'll get separate boats.

She laughed.

As they climbed the hill she noticed how the trees up top looked brighter than the ones below. At first she thought it was the sun. But the sun had set.

At the top of the hill lay an overturned truck, engulfed in flames. People huddled on the shoulder, one of them holding a hand. His own hand, in fact. A cigarette dangled from his mouth. After each puff he lifted what remained of his forearm. Out of habit, she figured.

Behind the truck were two cars, one humping the other. A cop appeared, waving them on. He looked embarrassed.

She reached for her cigarettes. Well that was intense.

Did you see anyone inside? he asked.

Didn't notice. A couple of beats later. There was a guy on the shoulder. I'm not sure but it looked like he'd lost his hand.

I know, I saw.

Do you think they can reattach it?

No answer.

She wondered if he was thinking about the concert, the soldier in the first row, his sleeves pinned at the elbows. I saw a guy at a fair once. A bass player. One arm, but he could play.

Traffic had eased, though the car in front was lagging. She could tell it was getting on his nerves.

He pulled out to pass.

She held her breath and thought of her mother.

He took his time re-entering. When he did, he turned to her. If something like that ever happened to me, I'd want you to do the right thing.

[8×10]

What's that?

Put me out of my misery.

Too late.

I'm serious!

I know you're serious, she said to the window. Just keep your eye on the road.

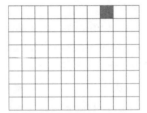

A week before his retirement he was visited by a woman whose father had been a client. She told him his name, but he had no recollection. She described his appearance—still no bells. Then, from a shopping bag, she pulled out a suit jacket—and before she could retrieve the slacks, he remembered.

He held up the jacket, gave the lining a tug. Your father was an intelligent man. He looked at her. Intelligent but impatient. Always asking me to hurry up!

That's him, she smiled.

He picked up the slacks and checked the seams. Fussy too. In the trade we call a man like that a tab.

A tab? she said, reaching into her purse for a pen.

He held up the jacket again, this time turning it from back to front. Some puckering on the lapel.

What's puckering? she asked, writing the words *tab* and *puckering* on the back of an envelope.

Too much tension in the thread. I've always had bad luck with finishers. My son did this. He was a real bodger! And with that he cracked up.

She asked what a bodger was, but he was too busy laughing.

Laughing relaxed him. He did not like being alone with women, especially in the shop. Laughter put everyone at ease. Even a pretend laugh.

So, he said, putting the jacket aside, how can I help you?

I'd like to have some alterations made.

He nodded.

To my father's suit, she added.

Now he remembered. Not what her father looked like, but who he was, his importance. He was unsure how to proceed. But your father, he is dead, no?

Yes, dead and buried. A long time ago.

Then how am I to alter his suit if . . .

No, no, no, she said, smiling, it's not for him, it's for me. I want you to alter the suit to fit me.

The thought appalled him, yet he could not resist doing the calculations. If her father was six feet, two hundred pounds, and she was eight inches shorter and eighty pounds lighter, an alteration would be impossible. He would have to take the suit apart.

That's fine, she said.

It will be expensive.

Money's no object.

He took a breath. He was waiting for an excuse, something he could laugh at, but nothing came. He looked away.

Do you not want to do this? she asked, trying to catch his eye. Because if you don't, it's okay.

I've never made a suit for a woman before.

Then I'll be your first!

He chuckled. It was an honest chuckle, but it did nothing to relax him. I'm not sure I can, he said glumly.

Why?

Because women don't wear suits.

Some do.

Now he was angry. Not at her but himself. He kept glancing at the door, as if someone were about to walk in. He thought about asking her to leave.

Look, she began, I'm not interested in wearing the suit, I'm only interested in the scraps, the leftovers. I'm an artist, and I want to make a piece about difference.

He smiled weakly, wondering what his son might do in this situation. You mean the difference between you and your father?

Something like that.

So what will you make with the scraps?

She shrugged. I'm not sure yet. Maybe nothing.

He liked her uncertainty. But more than that, her willingness to share it. Do you think your father would approve?

In a way, she said, laughing.

Okay then, he said, smiling, in a way then it is.

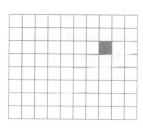

Look at my face, she said.

He looked.

Describe what you see.

Beauty.

Can you be more specific?

I love your eyes.

Why?

They're beautiful.

Describe them.

They're light, the colour of sand.

The wind picked up. A siren in the distance.

If I were missing, how would you describe me to police?

He shrugged. I don't know.

Pretend I'm a police artist.

Okay. She's about average height—

No, just the face.

Okay. She has a round face.

Go on.

Dark hair, kind of wavy. Long.

How long?

Over her ears.

Okay, now shut your eyes—but keep describing.

Her lips are full, her bottom teeth crooked. He opened his eyes and pointed to his own. Like mine.

[8×10]

Close your eyes.

He did. Tightly this time. Her chin is pointy, her cheekbones high . . .

Are you attracted to her?

. . . big ears . . .

In a sexual way?

. . . pierced.

How would you touch her, if she let you.

I would touch her neck.

Why her neck?

I would want to know how soft it was.

Have you ever touched a woman like that before?

No.

A man?

He opened his eyes.

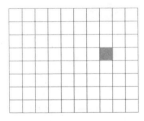

After his death, and what had begun to seem like an interminably long bereavement, one that kept her in bed half the day, prowling the supermarkets at night, eating ice cream for breakfast, she came to the conclusion that the only way to turn her life around was to retrace her footsteps until she arrived at the place where she and her husband first met, and depending on how that went, make her way back, renewed.

So she sold her gallery, left her home with a property manager and bought passage on an ocean liner whose route was identical to the steamer that she and her husband arrived on, but in reverse. This, she believed, would give her the impression of a life rewinding, as opposed to one that had come undone. Which, in her desperate state, was something she would be willing to settle for, an impression.

To reach her ship, she would have to take a train, a journey that took almost three days. It was while waiting for this train that she saw on the platform a young couple who reminded her so much of her and her husband when they were their age that she wanted to run up and tell them.

The couple stood crouched over their luggage, struggling with a case that would not stay shut. He was getting impatient, though she was the one doing all the work. Glancing at their baggage tags, she noticed they were headed to the same place. But unlike her, they were in second class.

After a series of well-placed bribes, she arranged for the couple to be seated at her table, in first. Although the husband was happy with their relocation, boasting it had everything to do with his being a doctor, the wife was suspicious, and she brought her suspicions with her.

You shouldn't look a gift horse in the mouth, he said to his wife, reaching for the butter.

The wife nudged her. Doesn't that expression speak to everything that's wrong with this world?

She agreed, but because she did not want to alienate the husband, smiled politely instead.

I mean, what does it matter how we got here? the husband added. We're here, aren't we?

The comment angered her, and in trying to manage her anger, her response came out mangled. If the means mean so little to you, Doctor, does that mean you would have taken a less expensive train if it meant that train was windowless?

But he did not hear her. A waiter had slipped. She assumed he was assessing the situation. Would his services be needed?

She smiled at the wife. But instead of smiling back, the woman glared.

There's nothing to say a train with windows would be any cheaper than one without, said the wife, her tone hard. In fact, I would suggest the opposite—that a train without windows would cost more to make, and therefore be more expensive to hire.

She was flustered. She tried to justify her question as hypothetical, but the husband interjected.

I think what the lady's trying to say is that I don't care how I get to where I'm going, just as long as I get there as quickly and efficiently as possible.

Is that what you're trying to say? asked the wife.

Well, yes, I suppose, she said softly, no longer sure where this was headed.

If her first night on the train was her best sleep in months, her second night was the worst. All she could think about was the couple, the way they played off each other. Why are people like that? she wondered. Are their lives so empty that their only chance at happiness is to compete with each other through strangers?

But despite the wife's behaviour, it was the husband she resented most. In reviewing what had happened, she wondered if his cruelty had become contagious, if he was the reason why his wife was so aggressive.

She slept through breakfast, and almost missed lunch. When she got to her table, the couple were just finishing.

You missed some beautiful scenery, said the husband, gesturing towards the window.

The wife did not look up.

Her appetite gone, she took a bun from the basket and left.

Later, while reading in the viewing car, she felt a tap on her shoulder. It was the doctor's wife. She looked upset.

I need your help.

Of course, she replied.

Returning to her sleeper, she took whatever cash she had and tucked it into an envelope. She was halfway through writing a cheque when she heard a knock. Just a moment, she called out. But as the words left her mouth the door opened. It was the doctor.

I apologize for the intrusion, he said, locking the door behind him, but I have to talk to you. It's about my wife. She's not well.

I'm not surprised, she said, getting to her feet. She reached for the door, but he blocked her.

Please, he said, just hear me out.

If you don't leave this minute, I am going to call the porter. Please, he said.

She relented. But only if he kept the door open.

My wife is in a dangerous place, he began, she has been under a great deal of stress and I fear she is on the verge of something extreme. He reached inside his coat and removed a letter, which he proceeded to read.

She could not believe what she was hearing, and after he had finished, said as much.

He handed her the letter. It was written on hospital stationery. She scanned it, then passed it back to him.

I'm sorry, she said, I had no idea.

He got to his feet. No need to apologize. The best thing to do is pretend we never spoke. Give her the money, and I'll return it to you before she disembarks. Someone from the hospital will be waiting.

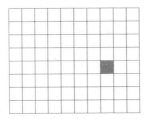

Two explosions, eight seconds apart. He counted to ten before the third one, another minute before heading outside.

The house across the street had been hit. Someone was already on the scene—a girl, moving through the dust, kicking at the wreckage. His first thought was to shout, They're not home, but he knew what she was after.

Two days earlier, the occupants had hired a moving truck. Everyone pitched in—parents, children, grandchildren. Over eighty boxes, all identical. As for the larger stuff, it remained inside. Whatever left the house left in a box.

The girl found an opening. When she got to her waist, she turned around. The fuck you looking at?

He thought of his daughter, the last time he saw her—posing for a photo beside him. Then he recognized the scar.

The girl's home had been bombed, too, but this was years ago. According to legend, the explosion was so great it blew her grandmother's glasses from one end of the house to the other, branding a semicircle above her left eye.

As for her house, it was not rebuilt. The decision to leave it that way had less to do with money than politics. The town wanted a memorial, and it helped that there were no survivors.

Then, about a week later, someone crawled out of the wreckage. The girl.

No one spoke to her, though her presence was felt. People began leaving food and toys outside their doors. Every now and then she would take something. A ghost who reminded, but did not frighten.

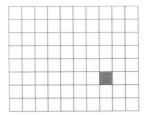

[8×10] Dinner was excellent, on that they agreed. He had the fish, she had the chicken. After that, a bowl of ice cream, which they shared.

The restaurant was a mile from her apartment, next to a bar where he once worked. Usually they took a cab, but on this night the air was warm and they decided to walk. As they passed the bar he turned up his collar.

They were a block from her door when he noticed a gang of soldiers gathered at the corner. One of them asked for ID, while the rest took turns throwing a knife at an over-turned box. She must have noticed, too, because suddenly she was motioning towards the alley.

This way, she said.

The evening had gone well; the last thing he wanted was a confrontation. Maybe we'll have sex, he thought, and with that he imagined her stepping out of her underpants.

They were halfway down the alley when something caught her eye. Look, she said, and as he turned his knees gave out, the back of his head landing hard against the pavement.

The next thing he knew she was naked. Crouched behind her, a man with his pants down. He did his best to get up, but someone was sitting on him, a woman. He could hear her breathing, and the soldiers down the street shouting for a cab.

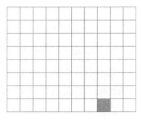

Arguments upset him, made him sleepy. When he felt one coming on he would ask to lie down. He knew it had something to do with his childhood.

His parents fought constantly, and their fights had a way of getting inside him. At one point he stopped eating, but that only weakened him for future arguments. For years he contemplated suicide.

Then one day his parents went at it so hard his mother grabbed a knife and stabbed his father in the shoulder. After that he went numb. His father was shipped overseas, came back, only to kill himself a week later. His mother sent him to live with an aunt, where he developed insomnia. Eventually the feelings returned, and he was drawn to the arguments of strangers.

He took his lunch in the stairwell of a building across the street from where he rehearsed. A medical building devoted to secondary branches of medicine—nutrition, rehabilitation, psychological counselling. Because marriage counsellors took up the third and fourth floors, those were the wells he ate in.

A typical situation involved a couple leaving a session, only to stop at the elevator and resume the argument that led them to counselling in the first place. The weakest spouse would head for the stairs, followed seconds later by their partner.

The stairwell was where the real battles occurred, and on a couple of occasions he got close. It was then that he started defecating on the third- and fourth-floor landings.

The introduction of a base material, he reasoned, would threaten the argument, create new possibilities—peace even. But as he soon found out, couples at that stage were usually so hostile towards each other that while one would start retching, the other would declare the smell ambrosial.

He had almost given up when one day a woman came bursting through the door, her hands covered in blood.

Oh my god, what have I done! she kept saying.

From there he followed her to the parking lot, where he snuck into the bed of her truck. He curled up on his side, as close to the cab as he could.

Eventually the towers gave way to sky. And soon after that, the smell of manure.

The truck made a hard left, and he felt the road change. They were on gravel now, and he could hear the sounds of children playing. Suddenly they came to a stop.

As the door opened, one of the children called out, Mommy!

Everything's okay, said the woman, we don't have to worry any more.

Why are you covered in blood? one of the children asked.

I helped a cow have a baby.

I want to see it! said another.

Later, said the mother. Let's get inside first. I have something important to tell you.

He waited for the door to shut before poking his head up. It was just as he pictured: a farmhouse surrounded by sprawling green fields. He climbed off the truck and started down the road. He was numb, and could hardly wait to get back.

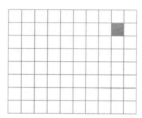

While flipping through the paper she came upon an interview with a retired soldier, a veteran of numerous campaigns. The questions were short, the responses long and gripping.

After reading it, she wanted more. So she read the piece again, and in doing so realized that wanting more had less to do with volume than what was implied, between the lines, in code. Or so she imagined.

Reaching for her pen, she began:

What was left of the town lay at the bottom of seven tree-lined ridges, between a sandstone cliff and the water's edge. Intelligence had declared it abandoned, but he had heard declarations like that before. Abandoned meant no one was around, although sometimes it meant snipers.

His mission was to secure the dry dock. Reinforcements would be brought in by boat. Once gathered they would circle the town and work their way in, cinching it.

Snipers aside, it was not a difficult mission. His last three were similar: cleanup jobs, more social work than combat. If he was going to make an impression he would need a bigger gig, and fast. There was talk of the war ending. He would have to raise the stakes.

[8×10]

Command had offered him two squads. He told them he could do it with one.

One! said the commanding officer, sitting up in his chair. One!

Yes sir, one.

Are you sure?

Fairly sure.

Fairly sure!

I mean, yes sir, I'm sure. I can secure the dry dock with one squad.

The officer gave him a hard look. Then, as if on second thought, he opened his case and removed a file, handing it to him. This is not a negotiation, son. This is a shitty little town we're talking about. Whoever goes in there will need all the help they can get.

He opened the file. On a typewritten page were the names of local officials, a recent census, and on the other side, a map. The rest were photos. Public floggings, a firing squad, a young woman's head stuck to a post. She looked ecstatic, as if the last thing she saw was her maker. He envied her, for he knew where this was headed.

There's nothing wrong with ambition, said the officer, his hands clasped before him. But putting good men at risk—that is not the road to promotion.

Yes sir.

Sometimes going into a situation a man short can mean the difference between zero casualties and total annihilation.

Yes.

The officer gave him another hard look before reaching into his case a second time. Do you know what this is? he asked, holding up an envelope.

No sir, he lied.

It's your recommendation. I wrote it last night. You know what I'm going to do with it?

No sir.

I'm going to destroy it. You know why?

Yes sir.

Why then, soldier?

Because I've shown poor judgment.

The officer reached for his lighter and held it to his pipe, puffing. There's something else I've changed my mind about.

What's that, sir?

I'm going to have you charged with insubordination. There's no room in my outfit for egomaniacs. Going into battle one squad short—what the hell do you take me for!

But before he could answer, the officer was on his feet, circling him. With his mouth an inch from his ear, he shouted,

If I ever catch you pulling a stunt like this again, I'll have your head on a post too! You hear me, soldier!

Yes sir!

I SAID, DO YOU HEAR ME SOLDIER!

SIR, YES SIR!

[8×10]

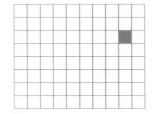

No sooner had she touched her glue gun to the angel's wing than the garage flashed white with light.

One steamboat, two steamboat, three . . . A dull rumble, then a loud crack.

Three miles, she said to herself, placing the angel on the bench before her. Three miles give or take. She wondered where the lightning struck, and when it might strike again.

Another crack. But this time no flash.

Curious, she looked towards the door. All of a sudden, what sounded like a canvas tent being torn in half. Then the roof lifting off!

She scurried under the workbench, burrowing between a lawn chair and a spare tire, the contents of the bench ricocheting off her back.

When she awoke, she was clinging to the bedpost. Her throat hurt, and she was covered in sweat. A tap was running.

You're still having those nightmares, he called out from the bathroom.

What was I saying? she asked.

If you took a pound of vowels and ran them through a meat grinder, you'd be close.

She sat up, peeked through the curtains. It was still dark. Come back to bed, she said, followed by three steamboats, I want you to hold me. She counted three more before tip-toeing towards the half-open door.

She could see him in the bathroom mirror. Naked, his buttocks clenching. Like a bellows, she thought. He was standing by the sink, masturbating.

He's bored with you, a voice whispered.

She covered her ears, but this only made it echo.

They had met in the park. He asked about her dog, and she told him. For an hour they talked. Art, politics, the war. As he got up to leave she asked if he lived nearby. Not yet, he told her, but I'm looking.

She returned the following day, same time. Her heart jumped when she saw him—sitting on a swing, reading a newspaper. She wanted to let go of her dog and jump in his lap.

That was six months ago.

Now all they had in common was her money. Was she as bored of him as he was of her? She pretended to give it some thought.

She remembered what her friends had said. He's using you. He'll only break your heart. You're old enough to be his . . . grandmother.

If he was using her, it was only because he wanted to improve his situation. Nothing wrong with that, she thought. She did something similar at his age, leaving her people for a better life. Was her return not to invite revenge?

He had talent, she liked his drawings, she could help. Was she a fool for getting involved with someone who might hurt her, someone young enough to be her grandson? Too late, she reasoned, her heart was already broken—and you have to have children to have grandchildren.

As for what he had given her—friendship, camaraderie, the best sex ever—it was still operative, and always would be, as memory.

All she had to do was think of him, and she felt better. Was it so important that he stay in her life, a physical reminder of what she already knew, and had, in the way that having something is supposed to make you happy?

His hips jutted forward, followed by a low, extravagant groan.

She pulled the covers over her head and whispered to herself, What a waste.

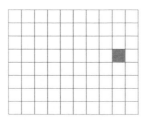

Something wrong, sir?

He was staring out the window, his plate before him, untouched.

The waitress tapped him on the shoulder. Sir?

He looked up. Not the girl who took his order, but her opposite. I'm sorry, he stumbled, I was just—

Take your time, she said with a smile, no rush. She refilled his cup, her eyes on the table ahead.

He returned to the window. It was a cool blue morning and the trees on the boulevard shivered. At the base of each, a patch of snowdrops. Like the mats he stood on at the hospital, when performing an operation.

A small four-door pulled up next to his coupe. A woman and her daughter got out and walked quickly towards the gas station. He reached for his utensils, cut off a piece of bacon and poked it in his mouth.

Next time he looked he saw a man inserting a key into the trunk of the woman's car. Navy blazer, grey slacks— that was him!

The man opened the trunk and withdrew a black briefcase. With the same fluid movement, he unlocked his coupe and slid the briefcase inside. Another bite and he would have missed it.

He looked at his watch. Traffic permitting, he would still have time to earn that briefcase before joining his wife on the evening sailing.

Everything okay? said a voice behind him.

Startled, he turned around.

The first waitress.

Just the cheque, he said, scanning the restaurant, her opposite nowhere in sight.

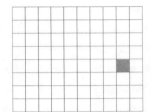

[8×10]

Birds woke her. New birds! Spring birds! All winter long, nothing but crows. And now these! Robins, chickadees, and when summer comes along, hummingbirds!

She decided to make a feeder. When he dropped in, she would be busy, and he would notice.

His last visits had been less than friendly. She would tell him about her day, and he would look at her as if to say, Don't be an idiot, we both know why I'm here.

A knock.

She put down her scissors and began counting.

Another knock.

Coming! Six, seven, eight . . .

She stopped at the mirror, to check her hair.

Furious knocking!

Sorry, she said, turning the lock, I was just—

He brushed past her, glancing up the staircase before storming down the hall, scanning the rooms as he passed them.

As he neared the dining room, she said, Hey, I wanna show you something? but he did not stop. When he reached the kitchen he opened the back door, poked his head out, then turned around. The fuck took you so long?

Unable to contain her excitement, she grabbed his hand and led him back to the dining room, where he went straight to the drapes, sweeping them aside.

No, on the table.

He looked at the feeder. The fuck's that?

For hummingbirds!

He looked at her as if she were out of her mind. What hummingbirds?

The ones that'll come this summer. She picked up the feeder and offered it to him. Here.

He took it gently, turning it slowly in his hands.

I used a water bottle and a plastic lid.

I can see that, he said, running his finger over the spout.

Careful, the glue's still wet.

Don't worry, he said to the feeder. We'll put it somewhere safe, where it can dry.

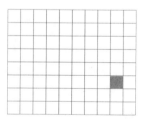

She rolled over. What just happened?

He took a drag off his cigarette. We had sex.

No, what exactly.

What do you mean, what exactly? You were there, weren't you?

I want your version.

My version? What are you, a cop? He took another drag off his cigarette, then dropped it down a beer can. Tsss. Is there a right answer to this?

She stared back at him.

[8×10] He recognized the face. I don't know, he began, we took our clothes off, went into the bedroom. I went down on you, you went down on me. I put it in, you—

How did you put it in? What position?

I was on top. You were wet and—

Good! That's the kind of detail we need—I was wet. What about you, what's the masculine equivalent of wet?

Hard?

Yes, she said, getting on her knees, hard. But how hard?

Where is this going?

Not as hard as when you put it in me later, that's how hard!

Forget it, let's eat.

No, answer the question, she demanded.

You've already answered it!

What happened after you put it in me, when you were on top?

We did it for about ten minutes, then—

Five minutes.

Okay, whatever, five minutes. Then I turned you over and put it in you from behind.

Yes, but how? Did you shove it in or did you start with little strokes and work your way up?

About eight or ten little strokes then—

More like four or five before the first big one. Or at least the ones you grabbed my shoulders for, which I consider the beginning of the first big—

So what you're saying is, you would have liked more little strokes.

I'm not saying anything, I'm just trying to get the facts straight.

Why?

Because I want to know if what we did meant anything to you.

Ah c'mon, you know what happens when people have sex, they go to different places. Time, space—all that shit gets abstracted.

Not for me it doesn't. Everything that happens is important. Everything means something.

He jumped out of bed. Water?

I'd like some answers first.

Answers or facts? he shouted back.

All I want to know is, how many big strokes did you give me before turning me over and coming on my face?

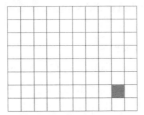

A nurse was adjusting something above her head. She could smell fresh flowers, but could not place their scent. Someone had come to see her, someone who knew her. The flowers smelled like they might be her favourites.

She blinked and the nurse turned into a gang of medical students.

Someone asked if she was conscious. Before she could respond, a voice from the back announced that she was in a vegetative state, and would someone care to start. A student stepped forward.

The patient is approximately thirty-five years old, a former intravenous drug user. The student pulled back her bedsheet. Note the scar tissue on the ankles and groin.

Any idea when the patient stopped using? the first voice asked.

Could be as late as a year ago?

Based on?

Based on the healing pattern of the scar tissue. Plus the patient has shown no signs of withdrawal.

The crowd parted. An older man stepped forward, the first voice. The patient has shown no signs of withdrawal because she was never a drug addict. A closer look at these scars will reveal a pattern consistent not with drug use but of self-mutilation.

The student bowed his head.

So, the older man said, looking around the room, who wants to take it from here?

A young woman stepped forward.

The patient was injured three weeks ago during a police raid. A single gunshot wound to the left posterior cervical. The bullet entered the midline anterior aspect of the neck, exiting the left posterior—

Stop. Who's next? Again he looked around the room. No takers? You, he pointed.

X-rays revealed bullet fragments, with fractures at C4 and C5.

Hematoma?

A large anterior neck hematoma was present.

Carotid pulses? Someone else—you.

Palpable. But there were no bruits.

Good. Post-op?

Computed tomography of the cervical spine . . .

Too late. You!

Cervical spine and cervical and cerebral angiography. Cervical spine without contrast medium showed bullet fragments C6 as far down as T3. Fractures of the left transverse processes C6 and T2. Small bullet fragment lodged in canal beside left inner laminar at C6.

Stop! Angiography. You!

Thrombosed left vertebral artery . . .

Posterior circulation runoff and carotid system—you!

Normal.

Prognosis?

The room fell silent. She blinked, and they were gone.

[8×10]

If someone had told him he would one day take over his father's business, he would have laughed. But that was what happened—just as it happened to his father, and his father too. Though he never told his son the story of what someone might have told him, there were times when he wished he had.

It had been ten years since he last saw him. Then, one day, while hemming a pair of trousers, who should walk in.

Hey, Dad.

Had he not called him Dad he would not have known who he was. Calling him Dad froze him.

What's new?

What's new is almost ten years old! he wanted to say but pricked himself instead. I work half-days now, he told him.

Can I use the washroom?

You don't have to ask.

He could tell by his suit that his son had done well. But what had he done to afford such a suit, how many lives had he ruined? Suddenly the pain returned. It began with his eyes, running down his cheeks to his heart. Then to his legs, the soles of his feet, before evaporating, rising ghost-like, making everything around him opaque, uncertain.

He felt a hand on his shoulder. Dad?

He nodded.

Can we close up? I'd like to talk to you about something.

Put the kettle on, I'll lock the door.

In the old days, he would have put the kettle on and his son would have locked the door. But not now. Now he did not want his son anywhere near the door. It was then that he realized what he wanted—not having his son home, but having him home for good.

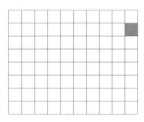

Winter was over, and with its passing, the realization that it could be his last.

He was doing the crossword, as he always did after lunch, when he began jotting down the places he had once called home, but in reverse order.

It would not be a long list, he thought. When he came to his war years, he wondered if he should count where he was stationed, like his trip up north, a time and place he was ordered to forget. He looked hard at the puzzle before settling on his three-month stint at boot camp.

In some ways, he felt more at home at boot camp than anything he had bought, rented or grown up in. Though not at the time, of course. At the time he thought he had died and gone to hell.

After doing the dishes he went to the hall closet and removed a box marked WAR. WAR was his oldest box, and had survived many moves. It was also his last to sort through.

He was familiar with its contents. Medals, commendations, souvenirs. What he had forgotten were the letters. At least ten of them, sandwiched together and bound by a cracked elastic.

The letter on top was from his sister. While rereading it he was struck not by what she was saying but by his remembrance of how he felt when he first read it.

He had just returned from target practice, disappointed with his second-place finish. His defeat, coupled with news that his sister had fallen in love with his best friend, set a fire inside him that took years to locate (and many more to extinguish).

There was a dance that night. One of his buddies had made a deal with the commanding officer: in exchange for cleaning the latrines, their unit could have the camp bus. Everyone pitched in, and the job took less than an hour. What they did not count on was that no matter how hard they scrubbed they could not get the smell off their hands.

The dance was at a town he had not yet visited. He had seen the others, but this one was by far the poorest. When they pulled up, everyone in the dance hall rushed to the windows, pressing their faces against the cracked and dusty panes.

The band was excellent. But he was not in a dancing mood, so he sat at the back, beside the woman selling pie. All he could think about was his sister, and that jerk she had fallen in love with.

As the band played on, his attention shifted to his buddies. His bunkmate in particular. A big, strapping lad—smooth, good looking, and as of that morning, the best shot in camp. If ever he had a rival, it was the guy in the bunk above.

His bunkmate had set his sights on the prettiest girl in the room. And to his delight, he was doing poorly. Every time he approached her, she darted off—if not to the punch bowl, then to help a friend at coat check. The more she avoided him, the harder he tried. And the harder he tried, the prettier she became.

The last time she avoided him, it was to help the woman selling pie.

He recognized her dress from a pattern his sister favoured. Not that he let on. Instead, he told her how much he liked it, how it differed from the rest, and how it takes courage to dress like that, what with the world being so suspicious.

The more he had to say about her dress, the more her face opened. And the more it opened, the closer it came to smiling. Until she caught herself. But instead of darting off, she thanked him—then left with the woman selling pie.

Nice one! said a voice behind him.

He did not have to look to know who it was.

I was this close to getting her dress off!

Back at the barracks, his bunk gently rocking, he imagined he was the one selling pie, and how happy he would have been to have walked this girl home.

With a chuckle he tucked the letter in with the others—when the elastic broke. He went to the kitchen where he kept such things, and noticed a truck lumbering down the hill. He had forgotten what day it was. Thinking quickly, he grabbed the garbage from under the sink, dropped the letters inside it, and collapsed on his way out the door.

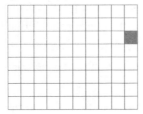

When they started, the sun was barely a sliver on her dresser drawers. By the time they lit their cigarettes, the shades had gone from white to yellow, and the room was blistering.

I'm gonna open the window. It's like an oven in here. He stepped over her, his cigarette dangling.

An ash fell on her stomach. She licked her finger, touched

it to the ash, then dropped it down the can beside her. Why can't we talk about it?

Talk about what? he said, struggling with the window.

What we were talking about—the war.

I've told you, he said, climbing back into bed, I'm not ready yet.

He took a drag off his cigarette, blowing the smoke low over his chest, erecting a nipple.

She got on her knees. When then?

When what?

When will you be ready to talk about it?

He shrugged. When I feel like it, I guess.

Wouldn't it help to start now? It's been a month.

A month and a half. And no, I don't need the help. Thanks.

He stared at his cigarette, now down to its filter. She took it from him.

Have you made any plans? she asked.

I'm gonna go to school, be a teacher.

Really! What will you teach?

I don't know. A bit of everything, I guess.

She put her hand on his chest, rolling her thumb over his nipple until it softened. What can you teach me about the war? she asked.

That it's unlike anything you could ever imagine.

She smiled. It's not like a teacher to put limits on a student's imagination.

He asked for another cigarette, and she gave him the pack.

Do you think there's a limit to my imagination? she asked.

No, but if pressed, I'd bet against it. For your own good, of course.

I'm hurt, she said.

Medic, he whispered.

After breakfast he cleared the table and washed the dishes. Coffee was ready, so he brought her a cup.

[8×10]

Tell me one story about the war, she asked. It doesn't have to be a story, you can describe an event, I don't care. I just want to get a sense of it.

He frowned. A sense of it? He thought for a second.

It's daybreak, my second month in the field. I'd just been reassigned to a squad patrolling a swamp, and I'm waiting for them to return. After an hour or so they start to trickle in. I can tell by their faces that something bad has happened. No one's saying a word.

The last guy is carrying a dog, a big old ugly thing, its head the size of a boulder. He lays it on a table and everyone gathers around it. Somebody tries to feed it, and it nips him.

Are you okay? she asked.

Yeah, he said rubbing his eyes, I'm fine. Where was I?

Somebody tries to feed the dog.

Right, somebody tries to feed the dog, but the dog isn't eating. It's been shot. Then this guy shows up, says he worked at a kennel. He gives the dog an injection and digs out the bullet with a penknife. The next day the dog is up and running, licking everyone's hand, fetching sticks. As far as I know he's still there.

What's the dog's name?

He took a drag off his cigarette. Didn't have one.

What did you call it when you wanted it to come?

He took another drag. I don't know, it just did.

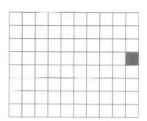

Pardon?

The woman at the till gave a quick look around. Then, leaning over the counter, she cupped her hand to her mouth and whispered, Come with me.

Now it was her turn to look around. Obviously the woman had something to hide. And if she did, she—not the woman—would need witnesses. She made eye contact with two businessmen sipping coffee at a newsstand. It gave her courage. I'm sorry, she said, but I don't feel safe. I've been conned before.

There's no other way, said the woman. You have to trust me. C'mon!

Is this what it has come to? she wondered. Risk one's life, all for an overpriced piece of cake? She turned from the counter, disheartened.

Suddenly the men from the newsstand were on her, their hands at her elbows, guiding her behind the woman as she made her way through the market crowd.

They were heading towards an unmarked door, between the men's and women's washrooms—when the woman veered right. One of the men ran ahead, grabbing her by the neck and pushing her through the middle door. A second later, she was pushed through, too.

It was just the four of them, in a small white room that stank of bleach. She had been in situations like this before, and based on what she was seeing, so had the woman ahead of her.

The woman began unbuttoning her skirt, when one of the men asked, What are you doing?

It's my good skirt, she replied, I don't want it ruined.

The other man laughed. Hey, if we wanted to rape you, we would have pulled it over your head! Ha, ha, ha!

The woman looked confused. So what am I doing here then?

The first man went to the wall and removed a long rectangular panel. She jumped back. A man was staring at her, bent over a sink, washing his hands.

Two-way mirror, he said. If you've never seen a men's washroom before, now you know.

Yeah, said the other man, barely able to contain himself, this is where all the dicks hang out! Ha, ha, ha!

They were told to stay calm and follow instructions. If they acted up, they would be killed.

Having no choice, they agreed.

Their assignment was to go to the men's washroom and wait in the last two stalls. Two men would enter and offer them money for oral sex. They were to accept the money and, just before fellating them, bite down on a capsule hidden underneath their tongues. The first man gave them their pills.

I don't understand, said the woman ahead of her. What are these pills for?

None of your fuckin' business, said the man who could barely contain himself. Just do what you're told!

Fuck you, said the woman, I'm not biting down on anything until I know what's inside.

Enraged, the man pulled out a gun and pointed it at her head. The first man intervened.

They were told that the pills, once in contact with the men's urethras, would set in motion a series of irreversible reactions, one of which was chemical castration.

She felt sick to her stomach. Not what they were asking of her, or that she was too old, but . . .

What about us? demanded the woman ahead of her. What will these pills do to us?

Nothing, said the first man, it's a guy thing.

She took a deep breath. Then, as if to herself, How bad does it have to get for someone to be treated like this?

The first man looked at his partner.

His partner looked away. There were tears in his eyes. These men raped our mothers, he began. They raped them, then they stuck their guns inside them.

You would be doing us a great service, added the first man. It is essential that nothing like this ever happens again.

She looked at the woman ahead of her. She was crying, too. But hers were not a prisoner's tears; they belonged to someone else. It was then that she realized what was going on, and how utterly desperate her people had become.

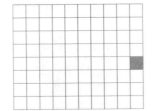

[8×10]

Unlike the other kids in the neighbourhood, whose fathers left for work in the morning, his got up from the breakfast table and retreated to a room full of books.

For the longest time he thought his father had something to do with these books. When asked by his teacher what his father did for a living, he told her, Books, and the teacher assumed he was a writer. It was only after she invited him to speak to his class that he learned his father was not the author of his books but used them to make his living.

I am a prospector, he told the class, opening a book and pointing to a bearded man kneeling by a river. Just like him.

A hand went up. You don't have a beard, someone said, and his father answered, Yes, it's true. Nor have I panned for gold.

Despite his youth, he was expert at recognizing confusion. He sensed it in his classmates, but especially in his teacher, who appeared frustrated by his father and on the verge of kicking him out. But before she could, his father held up another book, this one featuring a crowd of men standing on a floor covered in little pieces of paper, some of them pointing upwards and shouting. Then the teacher smiled so hard he thought the top of her head might fall off.

As he grew older he learned that his father spent his days buying and selling stock. And to help him, he read books. Not just mining reports and geological surveys but books on history, politics, human behaviour. When the time came, his father explained how it worked.

Everything has some form of value, he began, but only if someone wants it. If enough people want something, and there isn't enough to go around, the price goes up. If, on the other hand, there's a surplus, the price drops. The trick is knowing when to buy and when to sell.

Even these? he asked, pointing to his father's books. Yes, his father said, and he told him why.

One day, just before his graduation, he noticed his mother at the kitchen table, her head in her arms, bawling. He tried to comfort her, but she only cried louder. Confused, he went looking for his father.

He found him in his room, of course, leaning back in his chair, his feet on the windowsill, laughing into the phone. When his father saw him he smiled, gave him the wait signal, then quickly finished his call.

Guess what! his father said.

Why's Mom crying?

From now on your father is going to work like every-body else!

He looked at the books. But I thought you did this.

Not any more, said his father, bounding from his chair, brushing past him. Those days are gone. I start tomorrow.

Which he did, backing down the driveway at the same time as the dad next door. Mom, come see! he called out, but his mother was still in bed.

She was in bed when he returned from school that day, just as she was that night, and the day after, and the day after that, his father having left home for good.

[8×10]

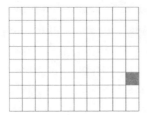

The best thing about being told she was dying was what it did to her sense of time. For most of her life, time was something she never had enough of: deadlines, being a wife, raising a family. After her prognosis, it elongated, slowing to a pace she had not known since childhood.

It was a hot afternoon, late summer. She was walking along the railroad tracks with nothing on her mind but the ripple ahead. Curled up in her pocket, a whip of red licorice, and in her hand, a bamboo switch, which she swung about her—whoosh! whoosh!—laughing at the sound it made. She was nine.

Your cancer is aggressive, the doctor told her. Unfortunately the treatment is not, and the results have been less than satisfactory. But if it's all the same to you, we should try.

We. She liked that. We can do anything—but I'm the one dying here! We. She flashed on the two of them gathering straw, jamming it into the cracks of a dike. Not her ideal wingman—she preferred her men strong, silent and aggressive. Like her cancer.

How long do I have?

The doctor shrugged. The survival rate is twenty percent after the first year. Of course the quality of that year must also be considered. If the tumours keep growing, your behaviour will be affected. To what extent, we're not sure. The brain is another planet.

She took a deep breath. If I could have a year, a full year, I would be happy.

Then let's try! he said, his enthusiasm catching her off guard, bringing tears to her eyes.

That was six months ago, she said, smiling. I have good days and bad days. Today's a good day.

Her daughter stood up and walked to the window.

You're angry.

Her daughter shook her head.

I was trying to be mindful of your situation. You were in the middle of a tour and—

Fuck the tour! her daughter said. Fuck it! Fuck it! Fuck it!

She sat quietly while her daughter scratched at her wrists, shifting her weight from foot to foot, her body a ritual of adjustments. She recognized the behaviour—she did something similar. But at fifteen, not thirty.

You've always kept things from me, her daughter began, until you find something useful. Then you wheel it out like a cannon. Do you know what I mean?

She knew. She treated her husband the same way. She knew he was screwing the woman across the lane, but why she waited twenty years to let on, him flat on his back, dying, was a question he could not stop asking. Why are you telling me now? Like their daughter the night before, on the phone, Why didn't you tell me sooner? As if it makes a difference.

I mean, is it revenge? her daughter asked. Waiting until the last moment, and then, Oh, by the way, I'm dying, I've been given a few months to live? Is that it—revenge?

Why is it important that you know my feelings?

Because I love you!

Because you're just like me, that's why. When you look at something, you're only looking for yourself. And if you don't see it, you look away.

That's not true and you know it!

Course it's true! I've listened to your records. It's the same song, over and over. How can you stand it? She reached for her pills.

Her daughter watched her. You're supposed to take those at night, before you go to bed.

She struggled with the cap. That's what I'm about to do—go to bed.

She reached for the pills. Mom, it's three in the afternoon.

But it was true, she was going to bed.

After her first treatment, she devised her own method of

[8×10]

slowing time. Sleeping twice a day, for five hours at a stretch, was like having two days. Combined with how she felt after hearing her prognosis, a week was like a month.

So at this rate, she continued, the next six months should feel like two years. Two years!

Her daughter poked her head out the kitchen door. What did you say?

I said, Two years!

[157]

Sorry, Mom, I asked you what you wanted on your pizza.

She smiled. You know what I'd really like?

Aw c'mon, Mom, not now. I've got the guy on the phone!

A whip of red licorice and a switch of bamboo.

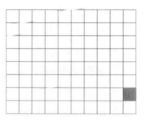

Who owns the train tracks?

The people who own the trains, she said, bending over to pick up a rock.

He eyed the rock. Hey, that's a nice one—don't chuck it!

Too late.

They watched as the rock glided past a power pole.

Almost! he squealed, his body tight with excitement.

I wasn't trying to hit it, she said casually, as if it were obvious she was aiming for the bamboo.

They walked on, the sun beating down on them.

If the trains own the train tracks, he began, does that mean the cars own the roads?

People own the cars, the government looks after the roads.

Yeah, but who owns them?

No one, the government does.

Who's the government?

[8×10] We are. You and me. People who pay taxes.

My father says I'm too young to pay taxes, and that he pays them for me.

Who was this kid? she wondered. She thought to ask him, but enjoyed not knowing. Let him do the talking, see where it leads.

My dad's in the army, you know.

What does he do there?

He kills people.

Did he tell you that?

No, my aunt did.

Your mother's sister or your father's?

My mother's brother's wife.

A bug whizzed past—a big one.

Hey, did you see that! he cried.

She had. It was a dragonfly. So who's your favourite, of all your aunts and uncles?

My aunt.

The one you just told me about?

Yeah.

How come?

He kicked at something, then picked up a rock of

his own. I don't know, he said, turning the rock over in his hand, she just is.

She liked his face. She imagined him grown up, getting out of a car, what he might be like in bed. Are you going to throw that? she asked.

If I tell you something, you promise not to tell?

Are you asking me or the rock?

Both, he said, looking up from the rock.

I won't if the rock won't.

He put the rock in his pocket and started walking. But faster this time.

She was having trouble keeping up. Hey, slow down, will ya. I thought you were going to tell me something.

I will, he said over his shoulder, but first we have to go to the secret spot.

She stepped it up, but so did he. She stepped it up more so. So did he.

They were nearing the bend when it occurred to her that the spot he was talking about had something to do with the tall stand of trees ahead.

A whistle sounded.

Her first reaction was to get off the tracks, look behind her. Nothing. As the train came around the bend, three more.

The boy was in full sprint, heading straight for the engine. She called for him to stop, but he kept on. Same with the train—until it ran over him.

Or so she thought.

As soon as the train passed, there he was, in the middle of the tracks, waving back at her. C'mon, he said. Hurry!

She could not believe her eyes. She ran towards him, faster than she had ever run before.

How did you do that! she asked, doubled over and out of breath.

Do what?

That train, she said, huffing.

What train?

[8×10] The train that just ran over you!

He took the rock out of his pocket. Do you believe in magic?

I do now, she said, catching her breath.

Hold out your hand.

She did.

He gave her the rock and asked that she put it in her pocket. She did that too. You're safe now, he said.

From what?

From whatever scares you.

She took the rock out of her pocket. It was orange, with grey stripes. You're scary, she said to the rock, and with that he disappeared.

Just then, another whistle.

As before she jumped off the tracks and looked behind her. Same train. But this time she could see through it, as if it were made of gas, not metal. She looked at the rock—it too appeared less than it was.

Feeling invincible, she stepped onto the tracks and ran as fast as she could towards the oncoming engine. Two more toots and she was crushed like a bug.

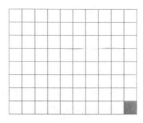

His childhood, when asked to recall it, centred on a single
event, an incident from which past and present grew, like
a tree. He was in the backyard, carving his initials into a
picnic table, when three boys climbed over the fence, one of
them waving a flag.

We're treasure hunters! declared the tallest.

And we've got the map to prove it, said the flag-waver,
waving the flag in his face.

The third boy, who was short and skinny and wore wire-
rimmed glasses, grabbed the flag and pressed it flat against
the table. The flag was their map, and he was their leader.
Here, he said, pointing to the X at the centre of the flag—
that's where the treasure's hid.

Surrounding the X was a square, and beside that, a tree.
Near the tree, what looked like a river. Or was it a road?

It's a river! snapped the tallest.

Which is why we're here, said the leader. We've come for
your canoe.

The canoe was all that remained of his father. It was
something he built himself, with his own two hands,
before he lost them in the war. A week after his return, he
went into the garage, locked the door behind him, and

died. By his own hand, people whispered, though he was never sure how that was if he lost both his hands in the war.

How do you know about my father's canoe? he asked.

Never mind, said the leader.

We know it's in the garage, said the flag-waver.

And that we're gonna get it! said the tallest, punching him in the shoulder for emphasis.

But it doesn't belong to you, he said, rubbing his shoulder.

Does now, said the tallest, punching him in the other shoulder.

He looked to the leader, for sympathy. The leader stared back at him, his eyes dull. He had never seen such a dead face. The difference between him and his cronies made him sick to his stomach.

After unlocking the garage, he was dragged back to the table where the tallest boy forced him to eat his vomit. Someone added a dog turd—when suddenly a car pulled up. Quickly they pushed the canoe over the fence, and were gone.

What's going on back there? his mother called out.

They took Dad's canoe.

Just as well, she said, checking his head for cuts. We'll be moving soon. Gives us one less thing to worry about.

His mother had been offered a job in another city. A bigger company, with better prospects. What came as a shock—what was harder to take than having to eat his own vomit—was that he would not be joining her.

I want you to live with your aunt awhile, she said. Until I'm settled.

But I've never even met her, he protested.

You'll like her, his mother said. She's quiet, like you.

He knew his mother had a sister, but every time he brought her up she changed the subject. It was not until he arrived at her house—a sprawling mansion in the middle of the countryside—that he learned her story.

According to the butler, his aunt was an attractive, intelligent young woman who, at an early age, fell in love with a much older man. Together they travelled the world and made lots of money. One day, while driving home from the city, their car was commandeered by soldiers. The man was killed, while his aunt was assaulted and left in a vegetative state, where she remains to this day.

As the butler told the story, the staff gathered around them—first the cook, then the chauffeur, the gardener, maids—all of them standing there, smiling. And somewhere upstairs, in a vegetative state, lay his aunt. The thought of her lying there made him sick to his stomach.

One of the maids rushed him to the washroom. While wiping him down she told him, very sweetly, that his response was nothing to be ashamed of, and to wait while she fetched a clean shirt.

Once alone, he overturned the wastepaper basket, stepped onto it and climbed out the window.

Ahead of him lay an open field. There was a farmhouse to his right, and to his left, a large stand of trees. Although the farmhouse looked warm and comforting, the trees felt safer. He knew if he reached them he would be free.

But the trees proved farther than he thought. And the light, which only moments before held everything so evenly, was fading. He was barely halfway across the field when he came upon a dip, at the bottom of which flowed a stream. On the other side, a willow.

As he drew closer, he noticed someone digging at the base of the tree. A boy, and beside him, his father's canoe. He turned to run, but who should be standing there but the flag-waver.

Shh! said the flag-waver, his finger at his lips. He can't see you, he's not wearing his glasses.

Then someone grabbed him by the neck—the tallest boy—and the three of them retreated behind a boulder.

What's going on? he asked. What are you doing?

Here, said the flag-waver, shoving a pair of binoculars in his face. Look for yourself.

He did not have to look to know who was doing the digging, but he looked anyway. Not to be sure, but to see if he was wearing the face he wore in his yard that day, and how different he might feel about him now if he was.